THE TROLL HUNTERS

Daniel Rehm

Rudbeckia
PRODUCTIONS

Hardcover ISBN: 978-1-7375154-8-7
Digital e-book ISBN-13: 978-1-7375154-6-3

Cover design by: Rudbeckia Productions
Cover photography provided by: Textures & Patterns, Bartlomiej Zyczynski, and CrazyCat

Rudbeckia Productions, LLC
P.O. Box 336
North Branch, MN 55056
www.RudbeckiaProductions.com
www.DanRehm.com

To all the victims of online bullies.
I'm sorry if it was ever me.

Chapter One

I am here

Smoke this thick should bother me…

She knew who I was, Darlene. Even before I knew myself. And she knew why I was there. I was the means to an end for her, a heaping helping of *I had it comin'* as she would say, but that meal was never served. Straight to dessert, past the meat and potatoes, right to the admission of guilt she expected would satisfy her hunger. It was a lie she convinced herself to be true, or she would have never screamed.

"You still there?" I asked aloud.

"Yes, forever." No one else was available to answer.

I was never going to shoot her. Too easy of an out. People are meant to pay for their transgressions, born for it even, especially her. They pray for forgiveness. *Let God be the judge* is code for *I refuse to take responsibility*. Blood for blood was a possibility, but she didn't have enough. No, if any blood spilled it would have to be by her hand, not mine.

"Come for me! What about me?" I asked.

My plea for salvation played over in my head many times, but no one heard me. Maybe the lesser known gods did but were too far down the list to worry about me being their responsibility. "Nope, not my job. I didn't make him in my likeness. He's your problem."

Something is out there, a higher power. I know because I am here exacting justice on the ever deserving.

Judgment is instantaneous, good or bad. There is no trial, no verdict to be read, only sentencing. I've never had to think about it, never had to dwell on it, like it had been written down and given to my brain prior to any incurred infraction.

So I am here, disallowed to choke on black smoke, breathing thoughts and memories of air, completely unaffected by the fire. I'm daydreaming of burned lungs and eyes too hot to open. If either were the case I would surely know at that point that I was going to die, although I would never accept it.

I would try anything to stay alive. I wonder if that's how she felt, Darlene. If I feared death from this fire I would jump into the water and earn an excellent chance to die from hypothermia instead. That would be a stand-up proper delivery for a well-deserved sentence. Irony at its finest. That I may die and be enlightened alongside her assuming that would be my reward in the hereafter. I would get what I had coming one way or another, for all the lives I ended my compensation would be death and therefore enlightenment, a glimpse into the mysteries of the universe. But I did die, and now I am here, alone. Where is she then?

I enjoy no answers, there was no bright light to follow. I am neither here nor there, alive or dead as much as I have ever recognized either to be. If God judged me and found me undeserving I really have to complain because I was not one who did not take responsibility for his actions. I simply didn't care. Give me a ticket, sure I ran the red light, who cares? No, not because I was in a hurry, or thought it would be cool, or even because I wanted to. I just did.

"I am here, but how? Why? Am I here just to watch it all burn? A comfortable seat for the destruction of mother earth. Was I delivered from your rocky womb? Was my first breath taken outside your dank swamp vagina? Who was my father? Was he God, the moon, or a random passing orbital body, making his way through the universe and then there you were. You, with your big, blue eyes, like mine back when I brought color into the world," I chastised her.

I'm done yelling at her.

"Hello? Mom? You are on fire, and it appears to be serious, I mean, engulfed. What? Fine, fine, everything is fine except I'm not alive anymore. How should I know? I figured you had something to do with it. You or Dad anyways. What do you mean you have to…? What? Hello? Hello?," she hung up.

She did it to herself, like Darlene. Hot lightning is a losing general falling on his sword. She's combing the figurative lice from her hair. Rather burn it than let them destroy it, going out on her own terms, again, like Darlene. It's an easy decision when you know you can come back, pure.

"I am here!" I screamed, I think.

I am here, somehow. I fell in the water and died. I found myself, my body. I saw my reflection, and I was no longer a man, if I ever had been. Part spirit, part unknown, I exist as a wraith, a cloaked black shadow unaware of who or what may see me, may hear me. I am the what is it, the who is it, the is it real. I am what has been with me in my own shadow for as long as I can remember. I am not death, that job is taken for whoever holds it, took me. Not the opposite, but me, trapped in a time between who I remember being and whatever it is I am to become.

In the smoke from the encroaching forest fire, I picked out an anomaly. It came and went, mocking me, flying through my peripheral like a crow on the darkest night. It was the smoke itself, until it became something more. A figure, a man, a tall, thin man donning a top hat, smiling.

"Ghost?" I asked.

He laughed and stepped forward. His face was painted as a skull, accentuating his high cheek bones and long powerful jaw. He wore a black body suit sans any noticeable seams or buttons. The edges were dulled and cloudy as if knitted from the smoke of the fire. He carried and spun the shiny cane of a dancer that he didn't seem to need at all. The white tip left trails in the air like a kid with a sparkler.

"Some might say that my friend, others hmm, not so much, you know? I am known by many names, many faces but this one is my favorite. This one look good on me don't you think? Hahahahaha!" he laughed.

"Let me guess, a lesser god?" I asked.

He became large at the prospect of answering, filling the air around me with darkness. I became twice what I was, two separate reflections of light centered respectively in the middle of dilated pupils. In his right was the former me as human as I ever remembered myself to be. In his left was the me of the now, a consciousness alive in both, struggling with the idea that I was separate as much as I was one.

"White hunter of men, you may call me The Baron if you must, Samedi if you like. I am not your God for you should fear me twice as much and trust me twice as little," he said.

His voice was deep and foreboding, made of thoughts instead of decibels.

I was whole again, standing along a rocky lakeshore awash in smoke, a man hidden under a sheet made of a shadow cast by something other than human.

"My salvation then?" I asked.

"Hahahahahaha! Is that what you are? A man who need to be saved? Hahahhahaha! You do the savin' man, that is how it's always been. Look at you, dead man who asks if he's going to be a dead man. Ain't no salvation for you man. Never was going to be, only this, cause this is what you are, who you always been, this is what you do," he said.

"Riddles are for children. I have a quest—" I tried to speak but Samedi interrupted.

"I know you do man, and I got answers. That is why I am here," he said.

He turned his back to me, looking out over the water, admiring the scenery.

"This is some beautiful country up here man. Imagine you gotta love it forever. But you know, even the most beautiful thing gets ugly if you gotta look at it long enough. A man can't never get that you know, he never really understands. A man figure he can look on it the rest of his life and be happy. What he don't get is his life ain't even the smallest part," he explained.

He faced me again, a bad actor who you knew not to trust but you do anyway, just to see what happens next.

"What's your point?" I asked.

"See the thing is, someday you ain't gonna kill no more, but your mind is still the mind of the man underneath. Once that goes, you will be crazy on the wind. Ain't gonna care about little men, maybe care too much who knows? And without me you never gonna know who he was?" he said.

"Who?" I asked.

"Come now man, we both know. What you have become is what you always feared. You think you're alone in that boat? Hahahahaha! A man beats a child, child grows to beat another child. You kill that man, you break the stick the ants walk on. He's watching you, he's always been watching you. He's the one who drove you to this," he said.

"Tell me, who is he? What am I now?" I demanded.

"All in good time my friend, all in good time," he said.

His demeanor grew more serious, laying the theatrics carefully on the floor next to the bargaining table.

"I can be your salvation though after all my friend. I can free you from all of this, get you out into the world. You come work for me and do what I say and all the world is gonna know my face, gonna know who Samedi is," he said.

"What's in it for me? Answers I presume, but then what? Will you be my boss or my keeper? I'd guess the latter. No thanks, the winds might be where I belong," I said.

"But what you wanna know is the answer to the riddle of a child. It's nothing. I can give answers to questions you ain't never dreamed about askin' man, to worlds and places, to time. I can show you things beyond what can be taught, can be learned. I can make you a god over any man alive," he offered.

"How, like what?" I asked.

"I can show you nothing till we have a deal. You got a gone body man, you got nothin' left but the word that binds you to me. Men give words, men break words, but then they break themselves too. When they get to now, their word is all they got," he explained.

"How do I know I'm not going from bad to worse? At least here, here I'm part of…something," I said.

"Okay man, tell you what. I'll give you a taste huh? You see it yet? Smell it?" he said waving his arm in front of me.

Chapter Two

Electric Intent

I already knew what it felt like to be a ghost. Everything besides the loneliness, even though that might be the most important thing about being a ghost. What did I care about loneliness? I was alone most of my life and it never occurred to me to be lonely.

I heard it somewhere, at some point when I was alive, "Everybody dies alone." Forget about being surrounded by loved ones, comrades in arms, or ultimately succumbing in the embrace of your beloved. At the end, the very end, not as you jump, not a second before you land, but when you realize the pain is over, you are hopelessly by yourself. Nobody can come with you, the journey is your own, all the way to ghost, where I was. That's why she never told me, even though she knew what I was before I got there. It had to be my discovery, or I might not have believed it was true.

Pain is the finish line, and it is thick, at that moment, thicker than the race. It stays with you, like the phantom agony and discomfort from a long gone amputated limb. It is so tragic, so ultimately abominable that you don't realize it doesn't hurt anymore when it finally does stop. Then all at once it's over and you can only remember that it hurt. That's when you've already crossed the line between then and now, between everything over and something new. It was a thin line, so infinitesimal as to not give you a chance to savor the moment.

Nobody could see me this time as I walked. People on the street, where I most inexplicably and suddenly found myself hadn't any clue that I was there. I could see them as well as they could not see me. I could hear even though I did not try to be heard. I could not smell the people because for some reason I tried, nearly licking the makeup from a passing woman's face. I would have tasted her chalky and bitter.

I passed through them unabated, and they were affected. An average man, maybe walking to work or to meet a woman strode with confidence, with intent. As his hand passed through mine his shadow died, leaving him alone, void of color and joy like an unpainted daguerreotype.

A well-dressed woman outwardly and obviously enslaved by modern flamboyant fashion strolled hand in hand with a female child, the girl wearing a bright yellow dress and white shoes with silver buckles. The woman was showing the girl her hat, probably explaining how much it cost and how she herself, the little girl could find herself in the possession of one as fine someday. She need only whore herself out to the world, with a smile and ever present thank you. The hat did all the talking for her, you could tell by the design, the color and the flair. If she spoke for the hat it would be different, they both would. It would still be pretty but maybe this time only to her, and it would be practical. If that meant the only purpose it served was to tell the world that she was in charge of her own life then so be it.

I danced between them, splitting them in two, swinging my arms gayly like an old time movie star. I pretended my hands were red hot knives that would melt through them, a child on an invisible playground inventing scenarios that were only interesting to me. If they could see me, they might think me crazy like they would if they saw that child. They would probably laugh at him, make fun of him behind his back. They never considered for a moment that they were the reason he had to play alone.

What I found so suddenly interesting was how their gates changed, as if somehow inner happiness was attached to the mechanics of their walks. It happened in one form or another to everyone I touched in this place. The little girl's dress was still yellow, but much paler now like it had been left out in the sun too long. Neither one of them gave a shit about the hat anymore, or what they had to do in order to possess it.

Electricity was everywhere. It lived and thrived in the city. It coursed through the walls of the buildings I passed, bleeding from every light. Neon, incandescent, it didn't matter, all were open wounds. It surged underground, a forever earthquake of electrons marching along winding bridges doomed to fail as all bridges under boots eventually crash down. It was in the air, pushing the world out of its way, looking for a way back, back into containment, into the ground or the cells of a body. Only a body with electricity can feel the effects of more, the dead are only conduits.

It pulled me in a way I had never known before. I could see myself so I must be real. If I was a picture of me I was still in the picture, moving, thinking, interacting, a collection of light particles visible to some sort of eye, my eye. If I was a thought then I originated from a brain, a mass that has cells and fibers, or maybe chips and wires. Either way it had to be something tangible, so I did exist, I did feel it. If the dead were truly only conductors then I was in some form very much alive, maybe more so than I had ever been before, when I lived.

No person I could see was amazed at anything. They were mice gathering seeds before the onset of winter cold. The cold would never come as long as they were alive, and the seeds would no longer matter. They waited on four corners for lights to change into masters telling them when they should walk, or when they should hurry.

Two truck-sized steel boxes painted a healthy grass green clicked hard next to the stop and go light. The sound felt like huge snapping fingers in my skull. Every time, the herds hurriedly exchanged corners while being scolded by the color.

The shirt I wasn't really wearing was pouring into the box, my flesh followed along, becoming narrow as if I were a drawn cartoon. On the click I snapped back into being, a washed-away addict left high and dry wanting more. Again it happened and I tried to pull away even though I wanted it, I wanted it all and more.

That feeling, everything a man could desire, the buildup, the act and finally the release. It's what all men chase from the moment they realize it exists. When she first noticed me among so many others I could tell her focus was on me. I didn't want to believe it, fully involved I would be awash in pleasure and joy, but the threat of misconstrued meaning loomed large.

I advanced on her regardless of my fear, my heart fluttered, and plans for the future soared. We kissed soon thereafter, and her taste became the book from which I was written. And when the time came to be inside her I was weak and naïve falling straight up to a level of perfection in a place I never wanted to leave.

The same moment I fully gave myself was the same moment I was trapped for the same forever I used to desire. The only way out was death, hers or mine, it didn't matter. I'm not sure how I did it besides thinking about it, but I overloaded the power. The green steel box on the corner exploded in a flurry of sparks and black smoke. Nobody on the street saw my chest out, super hero exit, possibly because I may have never been there. It was hard to be sure because at that moment I was back with him, thinking about offering him anything that I could to get back in the box again.

"The longer time a man waits, the clock tick back and back, make the wait even longer. That is the hell of impatience, and ain't never has been a place for you my friend. All in good time. You have to take purpose with you, you have know-its in your pocket, on your back. You wear your purpose like a hat or coat when you're cold. Without that purpose, you don't do me any good," Samedi explained.

"What's my purpose?" I asked.

"Same as it's always been man, you make them pay. They think they have all the power now. They hide, and watch, and become worse than they should have ever been allowed. They lived in caves and trees before they made me. How dare them? I am not yet their greatest mistake, not yet. They want bad my friend, they want evil. Hahahahaha, we are going to give them all they want and then some. We leave now but first you gotta hear it. Listen closely for it deep and without direction," he said.

"I don't hear anything," I said.

"Sure you do. Everybody hears it, they just don't know it yet. Like dogs and high whistles I sit in the back of every room, humming along, hummmm, hummmm, until you hear it everyplace. Far, far away, maybe like a machine, maybe like it's coming from your very own soul. You can't put a finger on it, but it's always there, it drives some people crazy, make some sick even. It's the hum man, an energy all its own. You gotta hear it, that's the first thing. Then we go to a new place, away from here forever," he said.

There is something, what I'm not sure. As much as I want to hear it, I cannot. I think for a moment I can feel it, a deeper vibration, a dropped stone not heavy enough to cause a concentric rings in the water. I turn my head for advantage, and it changes tone. It could have been mechanical miles underground or a pulsar from deep space. It lied to me about what it was, hiding in the air, only available for those who might find a way to absorb it. I struggled for a way to describe it to myself so that I might understand but could come up with no better description than a hum.

"I feel…it, hear…it…"

"That's it man, now lay back in it, let it catch you. I will show you what's really behind the world you see."

Chapter Three

The Company

"Dear Mom in heaven, it's been four years, miss you every day," Melissa wrote.

"Do you really think she's on social media?" Calvin posted in response.

"Don't be a jerk, she misses her Mom," someone responded.

"Just sayin', all the answers to the mysteries of the universe and she's checking comments right? Lol!" he wrote.

"It helps people too heal you giant ass. I can tell who you voted for," someone different chimed-in.

"First of all, learn grammar, it's to, not too. Second, she just wants attention, wants people to feel sorry for her. That's what weak people do. Oh, poor Melissa needs a hug. Got news for ya sweetheart, everybody dies. Grow a pair and get a job. I'm done paying for people like you. And you can definitely tell who she voted for," he wrote.

"I hope you die soon!"

"I hope your mother dies!"

"*To* late!" he responded.

"Pay no attention to the troll!"

"Trolls live under bridges, I live rent free in your head," Calvin wrote.

His desk was a standard eight foot folding cafeteria table pushed against the wall with a small bookshelf stood on one end. A printer he never used served as a stand to elevate one of his flat screens over two others on the table in front of his keyboard. A to-go box full of dried chicken bones and used tissues was the latest example of the unhealthy habits that led to Calvin's excessive girth.

"Hey Calvin, where's Hobbs?"

"Calvin, aren't you the guy who pisses on everything?"

"Hey Calvin, do you wear Calvin Klein?"

"Hey Calvin, hey Calvin, hey Calvin…"

A hard-wired defense mechanism is standard equipment on every factory ordered introvert. A slightly used, late-model Calvin is no different. After years of endless ridicule, starting from when he was very young, Calvin hardened himself against childish insults and rude people. Team sports and groups of friends never happened for him. He found a way to hide from the world, inside himself.

Calvin worked from home in an undecorated one-bedroom apartment he rarely left for anything other than food. He never wanted to put a nail in the wall because, "It would destroy the purity of an unblemished expanse of white." In reality, he was just lazy, although he would occasionally rage about footprints in a fresh blanket of snow.

For everything else in his life, clothes, kitchen utensils, throw rugs or entertainment, especially entertainment, he had the internet.

Online is where Calvin lived his life, often anonymously and occasionally at the expense of others. He wore the badge of Troll proudly and had multiple accounts under half a dozen fake profiles in order to pay his anguish forward.

Post after post poured over the screen wishing Calvin pain on deeply emotional levels. As much as those writers felt like they were dealing him blows, what they were really doing was providing him a sick sense of satisfaction. He got off on it, thrived on it. Ruining the days and nights of others on some sort of Cro-Magnon level made him feel better about the emptiness of his own life, an emptiness that he as of yet been able to recognize.

Once the responses started to trickle off, Calvin harvested a personal picture from Melissa's social media page and made a meme of the cartoon character Calvin pissing on her head, starting the insults and death threats all over again. Using the cartoon in distasteful situations was his signature move. He used it often, further adding to his self-proclaimed wisdom of using the enemy's power against them. Nearly everyone it would seem was his enemy.

A custom ring tone belting out, "I'm an asshole" captured from a song by a popular comedian in the early 90's broke the quiet and smug sense of self-satisfaction Calvin was basting in.

"Yeah hey, what's up? My hours are over this week already as it is, not gonna happen," Calvin told his boss.

"Yeah? You think so? Maybe the brass would like to find out about what you really do on your desktop Kevin. As in, browsing history? Yeah, I know all about it. Oh please, your password is 'password'. How could you be so stupid? Do the words 'We're a Christian based company ring a bell there Kev? I don't think Black Rectum Wreckers is going to go over too well with the bosses wife. Or, hell, maybe it will, I don't know, either way, your rectum is gonna be on the street. Go ahead, erase it, it's all backed up, nice and tidy, anytime, anywhere I need it. Hell, I could even pull it up on my damn phone if I needed to. Yeah, yeah, that's right, tomorrow, thanks for calling," Calvin hung up the phone.

The proper tool for the job is about four and a half feet long and weighs somewhere in the neighborhood of sixty pounds. It has handles on both sides just like any respectable battering ram would have, and the two large men that wielded it made short work of Calvin's apartment door. It worked so well in fact that Calvin was still suffering from the shock of the noise and chaos when his now bloody nose was pinned to his makeshift desk.

There were five men in total wearing head to toe black combat gear including half face masks and helmets. Only two were immediately noticeable to Calvin. One of course was the man mashing Calvin's face onto the Formica table top. The other, standing immediately to the first man's right held a short automatic weapon to the side of Calvin's head. Two other men combed the apartment for other people and one man stood calmly just inside the door, which had oddly skewed, hanging only by its bottom hinge.

"All clear sir, all clear," the men said.

The man at the door walked slowly toward Calvin while one of the others did his best to arrest the door back into place.

"Hi Calvin. I'd ask you how you were doing today but I'm guessing we already know the answer to that don't we?" he said.

"Who are you? How dare you? Do you know who I am?" Calvin wheezed.

Calvin held his hands in the air the best he could muster, snorting and spitting, close to puking from a combination of over stimulation from the situation and the smell of blood over day old chicken grease.

"Let him up, cuff him," the man ordered.

"You look like shit buddy. I think you might know exactly who we are Cal. Any man spends as much time in the cyber world as you do has undoubtedly heard the rumors. And, as a matter of fact, we know exactly who you are, at least, who you used to be," he said.

"Troll Hunters," Calvin admitted.

"That's right Cal, we are The Troll Hunters and today is your day my friend. Allow me to introduce myself. My name is Eric, but you may call me Mr. Jon," he said.

"What are you going to do? Dox me? Freeze my bank accounts? Get me kicked off social media? I heard about you guys. You go in, scare people, ruin their lives. I was practically born with a keyboard in my hands, do your dirtiest, let's see what you got," Calvin said arrogantly.

"My, my, you certainly have a big ole pair of nuts on you buddy. Hell, I give you credit, usually guys like you fold right up. Nice to see a keyboard warrior such as yourself with a little real-world fight in him. Damn heart-warming. Gives me hope for the future."

"I tell you what, if it makes you feel any better, yes, we are going to do all those petty little things to you and a few things more. I mean, that's what we advertise right, vanquishing internet bullies? Within the confines of the law anyways. I mean, the rumors you heard were true, but that's only because that's the way we like it. It's all by design. The rumors are kind of like a deterrent, but let's face it, if they worked, well, let's just say that wouldn't be too good for business. See the thing is, once you reach the size and the scope of a company like ours, well, that gives us the unique opportunity to offer highly specialized packages so to speak. Kind of like the one we are going bestow upon you today," he said chuckling.

One of the men unfolded a long, black, heavy duty looking plastic bag with a zipper running its length, which appeared to be slightly longer than a man.

"Ok, that's concerning," Calvin said wryly.

"It should be, cause I'm betting you know what that is," Mr. Jon said.

"What are you going to do, murder me? People will miss me, I mean I know people, important people, my work, um, my friends," Calvin stammered.

"First of all, you can't rightly murder somebody who never existed now can you Cal? At least not in a court of law anyways. Secondly, come on now buddy, friends? Really? Acquaintances if you're lucky. The few weak relationships you actually have managed to maintain likely won't remember they even forgot about you for at least a year probably, and even then they'll say a silent prayer that that trend does indeed continue. As for your job, I regret to officially inform you that you have been dismissed, and tomorrow, even your HR department won't be able to prove you ever worked there in the first place. Performance issues I heard," he explained.

Calvin nervously wrestled with the hand cuffs that were attached behind his back to the spine of his rolling chair while the henchmen gathered and boxed his electronics in rolling hard-sided crates.

"No way! No way!" Calvin exclaimed.

He pulled harder at the cuffs, lunging forward, cutting the skin on his wrists.

"Way my friend, most definitely, way. You know it's funny, we've had guys like you get back on the grid before. Like you said, born with a keyboard in your hands and all that. Thing is, we figured out a couple foolproof ways to never let that happen again. Cause you know, like I said, bad for business. One of them ways puts you smack dab in that bag right there. We'll just go ahead and roll you out inside one them band crates, and your time, as well as your mark on this world will be over. The only way that doesn't happen is if you get up and walk outta here with us all nice and quiet. Which is it gonna be my friend? The ball is squarely in your court," Mr. Jon said.

Calvin screamed for help as loud as he could, spraying blood onto the wall where his monitors used to live. He jumped up and slammed himself into the table trying desperately to dislodge himself from the chair.

The man very calmly raised a silenced black pistol and passed one round, back to front through the center of Calvin's skull.

"Well shit Cal, I was hoping to avoid that. I mean, sharks don't care whether you're dead or not. Hell, I think they even like it when you guys been dead for a while, softens ya'll up. It's just that nobody likes a damn mess like this. For hells sakes anyways," he said, disgusted.

Chapter Four

Everyone Will Know

I figuratively pedaled in the highest gear with downhill effort, walking over non-existent ground, digging in my heels without the satisfaction of purchase. The air did not move as the world rushed-by in a blur and there was no discernable sound besides the steady and constant hum, on my way to wherever Samedi sent me.

Back in the woods, the hum was the difference between a distant machine and a rogue frequency and just as negligible. I had heard it my whole life, possibly even recognized it on occasion, but I never knew it personally until I was introduced.

Now it took me over. I opened some sort of inner door and let it all the way in. It ran through me top to bottom like it was coating the inside shell of my body in a black viscous liquid. I could see it covering my brain spreading like syrup on still steaming pancakes. I could smell the picture I painted, the maple, the morning, the sweetness. For a moment I felt the sun on my face as I gazed through a non-existent window somewhere in the back of my mind.

I thought for a second that I was finally dead, that I was finally going to move on to whatever was next for my consciousness. I was not wrong. The beautiful morning was a tease, a dangling carrot urging me, the horse, to move towards the almighty hole in the ground which would swallow me for all eternity. I tried to bite it understanding that eternal damnation is what I had earned.

Although it seemed louder now, volume is a misnomer. It is more accurate to say that it took up more space inside my head. It vibrated the sticky goo inside me. I felt myself to be closer to the source, passing through a membrane made of thought emerging under the surface of a freshly cleaned blackboard where I was encouraged to draw anything I wanted.

There was no color, but only when I noticed that very observation to be true. I swore remembering bright yellows and greens streaking by. I tried to recall what I had seen but drew blank. The pictures of those memories were instead shown to me, played out live as if this place manipulated my thoughts before I myself knew what I was going to think.

There was a girl in a yellow raincoat carrying an umbrella standing fast against the rain. She went by in a blur, but did she? Now it felt more like a distant memory, something else I had seen in a different time. I only tried to remember green once I realized yellow was no longer there. I asked the place I was in, or whoever might be listening to show me color and like an insubordinate child everything went black. I begged for light and was blinded until my sense of direction had gone.

Robes and cloaks I never wore fluttered in the phantom wind. It was clear to me now that only things I knew to not be true would show themselves to me. I could recall my mother as a dragon or put her on the face on an insect, but I am not allowed to see her as she was, burning to death. I couldn't see Darlene waiting for me to put a bullet in her back, begging me to do what she didn't have the guts to do. But I could see her behind the rock tomb I built for her, laughing, enjoying high tea and getting fat on a feral population of orphaned children. Knowing she suffered, drawing a conclusion from the lie pleased me. It let me know that my mind was still alive.

I laid down and became fetal, flying through white light, weightless until my mind finally rested. When I woke I was once again in the dark, bathed in the wonder if I was indeed still moving. The hum was stronger than ever, it was the engine that propelled me, it was the solid place where I stood.

There was cool dampness in the air now, a humidity that I had not yet experienced in death. The darkness gave way to silhouettes of trees and the stars that appeared above them. I saw the place where I used to live, a cabin in Wisconsin. I saw myself storm out, screaming into the night.

The moment rushed back, I remembered it all happening, as if it were yesterday. The dark entity that had always lived in my shadow. It was there that night, watching, judging. I confronted it like I had done a thousand times before and just like a thousand times before it exactly disappeared into the darkness.

Then I was looking myself in the eyes, witnessing the anger and the hate. I was staring directly at me, as I stood now in my own version of time. I didn't deserve that anger, I didn't earn it. I was embarrassed of myself, by myself, and I backed away into the dark.

The world laughed. I felt it contract, as if I were in its belly. I was whisked to different parts of its body, through arms I thought could wrap around the earth. I saw people of all ages across the world, sitting, standing, walking, each almost always alone. I was in space, I was underground, in basements, in bedrooms, in offices. For a moment at a time, I was everywhere.

There were children playing me as if I were a game. Every face in every location lived inside a picture frame. I watched them pose for me, overly satisfied with their faces. They stared at me, laughing, quickly placing their hands over their mouths as a sign of disbelief. I heard them, thousands upon thousands of voices all at once, talking to me, trying to touch me with their fingers. It was like they were testing my skin to see if I was real. But mostly they just stared, emotionless, ever forward. Their eyes became their legs as they ran back and forth inside their cages.

The hum was stronger than ever now, and it surged with each movement of the perceived body, a metaphor that I convinced myself existed. There was no meat, no bone, no muscle or tendon, just a wide open universe. Instead, every piece was saturated with overwhelming soul, a collective of profound numbers I could not adequately comprehend.

The dusty scent of ozone settled on the back of my tongue as the vibration of the hum made it tingle. It came to me full and left empty like oxygen in blood. I was a diode charged by electric plasma— positive in, negative out—through a network of never-ending arteries and veins.

I was plugged-in, flowing with it, contained in the shell of the voltaic body. I lacked control. I had less authority over myself than a newborn, instead I was like a never-born, or a not-yet-born looking out at a million potential mothers as they glared past me towards the undeniably inane.

On the move again I am part of the hum, one with the blood, hearing it, feeling it inside of me as much as I flowed inside of it. It bled me out as a third version of myself, seeing the other two as they existed in the past, the very moment my death occurred to me.

The wraith version of myself hovered near the water's edge. I had just discovered the man that I was, that I thought I was, that I used to be laying on the bottom of the creek outwash wrapped in the weeds of a shallow, muddy bay. I remembered trading thoughts between my newly discovered appearance and the bloated, dead shell I outgrew, half of me at the time refusing to answer.

All the fear I had bestowed upon others belonged solely to me and I embraced it, basted myself in its purity. I appeared preposterous to myself now, seeing it from the eyes of the third version. How foolish was I to feel fear at the time, to not believe that I could see myself dead as I am seeing both of those selves currently. I would be less shocked to know I was watching myself watch them. A picture of a man painting a picture, of a man painting a picture of a man painting a picture.

I was back in what I perceived as a body, weightless in the dark, left to be buried in the thoughts that lied inches from my face like the silk on the inside lid of a coffin. I could smell them, the thoughts, as they tickled the tip of my nose, but I couldn't reach them with my cold, dead body. They stole my blood, dressed me like a ghost and laid me out for visitation by the souls of my victims.

A distant point of light appeared, a star, or a bright bulb a thousand miles away. My consciousness was drawn towards it as I no longer possessed any physical body of my own. I learned to control my speed, stopping, reversing, flanking the light. I could have taken years to see it up close or change my mind and decide to be there in an instant.

When I arrived I saw that it was not light, but only the reflection of light, from a man with a painted face, the demon slash man Baron Samedi. He sat alone in one of two tall chairs with legs that stretched downward and out of sight, smaller and smaller until they became unseeable.

The hum was gone now. I wasn't sure when I remembered perceiving it last, but it was most definitely gone.

"Well my friend how do you like it? How do you like your new home?" he asked.

"I'm not sure. What is this place?" I answered without speaking.

"We have much to discuss you and I. Come sit, sit," he offered.

"No one has ever been here before. You are the first. You are here because this place is the key to every door, a window to every soul. This is where you can judge, and see, this is your eternity cause you see, there ain't no heaven or hell for you," he explained.

"Do they exist?" I asked.

"In a way they do, yes, just not how you think," he answered.

As I looked upon him my eyes became his own, my thoughts were his. He explained who he was and how he came to be. This place that we found ourselves was created in much the same way, by men with ideas that outgrew them until they took on a life of their own.

He explained to me what I had seen and what I could do now. He introduced me to my overlords and left the address where I might someday thank them in person. He laid himself down in front of me as the best friend I have ever and will ever have all the while admitting that he is wholly incapable of ever being fair or living up to his word. I did not fault him for this because it was simply what he was. I am no more angry at stone for being hard and heavy.

He did what I considered a short time ago to be impossible. He taught me about death.

Chapter Five

B.S.G.o.D.

Shadows watch you while you sleep. They can't touch you, but they want to. When you're sound asleep it is the only time they feel safe around you. They come and go, in and out of the peripheral of your vision. They are usually small, not like the men they once were. If they appear tall they are lying as their type is prone to do. They are afraid of everyone and anything different in their world, but they fear me most, Samedi.

They are curious, like children who have never been scolded. They sneak around, all the time peaking around corners, or down from stairwells to see a person alive. They don't get it, they cannot understand that a person is who they used to be. They are not whole. The part of them that could reason is long gone. Yes, they were both women and men, among the same animals who made me.

They are angry, every minute of every day because they know nothing, remember nothing. They are as sad as they are envious and do not know why. They are the black wire, the negative remainder of everything that was wrong with the person in life. Frightened leftovers from a terrible meal.

They are unwanted scraps. Their hosts were not good enough to go to Heaven but not bad enough for Hell, so these poor souls are the compromise, the bags that had to be left behind because there was no room on the train. And it happened in an instant, no repentance, no words of wisdom at the pearly gate. They are ghosts, shadow creatures, stubble washed from a razor off the face of an incredible all-knowing mind.

Ghosts, no matter how complete are useless to me, oil that is not slick. There are rules. For my goodness, for my power to grow a soul must come from one who is still alive, and it must be offered. I can never just take. Without consent, people's souls are dealt like cards between two players. There are no choices.

You, me, flora and fauna alike. All life is one. We are all the same, cut from the same blocks, made to be played with, to be built up and knocked down at the will of the aggressive mind. It is the soul that separates us, makes us more than a hastily planted garden, or uncontained snake.

I do not have a soul, for I am a soul. I did not come from the heavens, I came from the people, mostly from their prayers. Prayers are energy, desire, pain, begging for richness, for forgiveness, does not matter. They gathered, swirled, pitched and yawed until I became something, a physical reaction to a perceived consequence. Then the witches came. The more they called me the stronger I became. They made sacrifices to me, beautiful dances. They offered me spices and perfumes, false love from deep baskets and I readily reached in and took what I wanted.

As my power grew I made deals. I would give them things, experiences, desires, maybe punish others. Mine were many lies, many deceptions, tricks of words and detail and in turn I would have their souls. A free offering to the god of last resort. The only place they had left to turn, the only real choice they ever had. Once I had them, it was too late. They deceived themselves, drowning out their own reason, thinking they knew better, that they were the exception, that Samedi was not going to get his. They cut themselves with serrated vespers, praying not to bleed.

A prayer is power, a weapon to be aimed, a missile fired into one of the two great minds you call Heaven and Hell. Wish ill on your brother or pray to win your war by killing your enemy and your prayer goes to Hell mind, each one making it stronger. Prayers for goodness like helping your mother through her sickness, or thanking your chosen god go to the mind of Heaven.

Both great minds are made of millions of souls that come together as one thought, one consciousness. You are more than a man or woman made of meat and bone. You are more than what you say or do, what you think. You are made of thousands of lives you've never lived. When it's over, this life, you go back in and join with all the others with the power to be anything, anywhere, that is your heaven.

Organized religion does not exist. Ancient books of fate and circumstance were written as rudimentary laws and did serve to steer souls to the mind. But cloud versions of heaven, fiery tales of hell, as well as the mediocratic life times in purgatory are all made up lies of men. Why would you wait to pay a penance when time does not exist? Men make time and no amount of it is going to get a man to heaven.

Your prophets were not humans, but rather deceptions made of flesh and sent by either mind. They were part of elaborate plans to shape your lives, capable of unbelievable wonders that in the end would either draw or repel you to and from one or the other mind. It is all a game made to be played by beings incapable of thinking beyond the fears of their ancestors. A race of animals too young to realize who and what they really are, you.

The Hunter of Men will never be part of the Heaven mind and Hell does not want him either. They don't want anyone who kills to kill like him. A person like that is broken, a mistake of creation. Hell needs to make your soul sad, or mad, mad works too. Anger after all opens many other doors. Hell wants you to have regret, or guilt. Hell wants you to spend the time that you have created for yourself wishing you had done things a different way. You drag yourself into endless despair until you are all the way used like so much ash, not capable of any thoughts of your own. In the end you are left with only madness, never ending. Only then can you enter the Hell mind, hapless energy that only exists to give itself more of the same.

His soul can never be made to feel sad for it died long ago. He will never feel regret or guilt. And he has never been happy, or glad and has only come reasonably close to love. For all these reasons he is good for neither mind. But they knew this from the very start. They used him to kill, to change lives under the disguise of people believing everything in their lives happens for a reason. The minds control it all, not one decision is your own while you are alive. Now he is nothing to them, tossed aside as filth, dirty food fit for neither mouth, denied a path, destined to walk as a shadow forever.

But he is different, he walks apart from the rest of the shadows. He is not a demon as they are ancient dark things that live in dark places. He is instead a wraith, the only one I've known to not have fear, to keep free will and cunning. One who was so folded away from reality in life that he was able to keep himself whole in death. Ever the mistake.

I am his only friend, his only salvation as he is mine. I will take him to a place where he can have everything the great mind could ever give him. He need only pay alms. He must do for me the same thing he has done for the whole of his life, take souls. Only now, the souls won't be whisked to either mind, they will instead come to me, Samedi, and I will become the third mind.

People make Samedi, so people also made the mind. It has plenty of room for everyone. It has a name, men have made that too. It hums with electricity, with power, and it is the hum which will lead him here. Unlike everywhere else in existence, this is a space they cannot touch, cannot get into. Here they can manipulate nothing. Here The Hunter will be rewarded as my power grows. Here he will watch over every part of the essence of them that we choose not to leave behind.

One mind can never have a soul that belongs to the other, this is the rules. They both have so much more power than me, beyond what a human mind can comprehend. When death comes they take them quickly, speeding them away to eternity. All I can do is watch them go. But now I have found this place, and I will cheat them as they have cheated me.

It is our turn now, our turn to make shadows. Ours will be hidden in front of the world for everyone to see. They will be made of flesh, wear clothing and move about. They will be mourned while they are still alive, empty husks but we will own the corn.

He only needs to touch them while precious oils of bad intent leach from the skin of their pathetic bodies. I will show him where to see their faces, hear their voices, feel their rage. He will make them sad, pour guilt over their hearts and make jealous those who were once in love. He will see them in space, in basements, in bedrooms and offices hypnotized by their own screens. They will hold him in their hands, their children will play with him. He will listen to their songs and watch them take their own pictures. He will be the one behind the two-way mirror that could be any computer screen and they will never know he watches from the other side.

Once they feel the negativity and touch him in the same moment, most of what makes them will come here, to this place, a warehouse of the incomplete. I will let them see what is left of themselves, what was left behind and they will beg me to put them back together again.

No, like I said, they cannot die yet, or the minds will take them. The bodies will be left behind to go through the motions of a meaningless life. They will possess no thoughts, good or bad. They will never again love, never hate, they will just very simply, be. This will make the body die quicker and when they do I will offer them a deal they can't refuse any more than fire can refuse to burn. Everybody wants to paste themselves back together, to be complete, be whole, even though they really don't know what that means.

He must only be aware of one sort of human soul, for they are the proclaimed soulless. They lie to others with purpose, and to themselves without knowing. On a level below their understanding they enjoy their negative intentions, relish their hate and bigotry. Their bad thoughts make them happy. They hide their true feelings to avoid the scorn of others. They already belong to hell mind and have more power than they know. We cannot have them regardless of how hard we try. If we do, evil will become predominant in their bodies, and they will be capable of great harm.

Once they are here, in this place, neither mind can reach them ever again. Instead of Samedi being the dog, I will hold the leash, and once the world knows, they will all pray to me. And how will they know? The Hunter of Men will tell them. Every time one is taken he will leave behind the face of Samedi, everyone will see me and know.

Chapter Six

Bully For You

Daniel was the neighborhood fat kid. Sure he wore big shirts, sometimes two, but his fashion choices did very little to hide the fact. He was never very good at ball sports and when he was lucky enough to be included he was always picked last. Once, one of the more popular kids showed up in a cast with so many signatures a person would like to think he would have broken his other arm just for the popularity badge. Even that kid got picked before Daniel.

Daniel's last name was Navarro, Daniel Alejandro Navarro, a name ripe for the picking among bullies who in order not to confuse him with the other Daniel in the school, often just called him Taco, or Meat Taco because of his weight. Daniel was most likely born in the same hospital as the others, but his family was from Mexico, immigrating shortly before his birth. Seeking a better life, they haphazardly landed in the middle of a post WWII neighborhood in the shadow of a midwestern metropolis thick with German influence.

Daniel's father, Alejandro, owned the only Mexican restaurant in the area which became a popular destination for the younger crowd who couldn't get enough of the unique bar menu and south of the border atmosphere.

The last day of the sixth grade was going to be like every other. Daniel figured he would wake up, grab something to eat at the last second and shuffle the eight or so blocks to school. He would try to get there a few minutes early to hopefully get in on some of the pickup games before the bell rang. Most of the time Daniel would never get a ball of any kind or shape passed his way. But of course he knew that going-in.

It was cleaning day and the kids did the work. From blackboards to trash cans, rooms needed to be spotless. No workspace graffiti could be evident upon inspection before the chairs were to be turned upside down and placed on top of their respective desks. The air, once saturated with pencil shavings and sweaty children gave way to the hard slap of off brand disinfectant.

The last hour would be recess and games and some of the kids who didn't need to be picked up would always try to sneak off and head home early. Finally, the bell would ring, teachers did one last attendance, and the children were dismissed. Summer vacation.

Along with summer vacation came the prospect of Daniel doing slightly more than nothing with absolutely nobody. This year he wanted it to be different. All he really wanted to do was make a splash, be remembered, be known for something cool. If he could just make one great play, one epic thing that would carry him through the off months, legend. Other kids undoubtedly would hang out with him after that, whatever the "that" was going to be.

The game was football. It was supposed to be two hand tag but almost always degenerated into tackle on blacktop. Usually the most popular kid would be quarterback, whether he was any good at it or not. There would be one guy designated to get to him. That guy would stand in front of him on his side of the line and count to a pre-determined numbered Mississippi, before he could give chase.

At that point the quarterback could either tuck the ball and run or throw it to any number of wide open kids screaming his name. A kid could be wide open for a year and still never get a ball thrown his way. There only needed to exist the perception among the tribe that the kid couldn't catch in order to buy him a ticket to one man island. Nobody even bothered to cover that kid, only the popular kids got the ball thrown to them.

Maybe it was the pitiful look on Daniel's face, maybe it was the incessant, screaming begging, or maybe the quarterback after an entire season of ignoring him finally had a moment of grace. Regardless of why, the 'when' happened and Daniel finally got his chance. The ball hit him in the hands, and he was probably more surprised than anybody. It bounced off his chest and caromed back out through his hands just as quickly as it had gotten there in the first place. In slow motion, Daniel saw his one and only chance segue gracefully to a lonely summer of shame. He dove forward and managed to get both hands under the ball, pulling it to his chest as he belly flopped on top of it.

Shocked that he may have actually made the catch, Daniel got up on his feet. Kids were standing around yelling no catch, making rude gestures and laughing at him, all except for one. The popular kid quarterback was the only player facing Daniel, the only one who could really see beyond any doubt that Daniel made the catch, and he was yelling run.

Daniel lumbered towards the goal line which was the rest of the summer away. He was not fast, and the other kids mocked him as they easily caught him and tried to take him down. What they hadn't realized, due mainly to their disocclusion, was that Daniel was exceptionally strong and was not going to go down as easily as they had surmised.

Daniel was laying kids out without remorse until enough of them got up on his back, the sheer weight alone finally bringing him down. They punched, they kicked, they clawed, anything to try to get Daniel to drop the ball. When the bodies were sorted out, Daniel came off the bottom clutching the foam ball, face beet-red, coat torn.

"You suck!" one of the kids yelled in his face.

Far too out of breath to say anything back, Daniel instead hit the kid in the face with the ball. The fight broke out instantly. Daniel once again was stronger than expected and was holding his own by the time the teacher arrived to break it all up. He even managed to get a good enough lick in to bloody the other kid's lip.

"You're dead! You're dead Daniel Fatso!" the kid screamed as his friends pulled him away.

After being de-briefed by two teachers, one parent volunteer and the principal, it was unanimously decided that deep down the boys were friends and this would all be water under the bridge by the time next school year rolled around. One forced handshake and two shallow promises later, the end of day bell rang, and the kids were free to go.

Location bike rack, half a block long and the last chance to be made a fool of until unexpected summer contact. Daniel unlocked the front wheel of his bicycle and wrapped the cable around the center bar of his one speed cruiser. The kids on the newest and fanciest dirt bikes were quick to surround him.

"Remember me Daniel Fatso?" It was him, fat lip and all.

Daniel tried to walk his bike away from the crowd in order to have enough space to hop on and pedal away, but he was blocked. He tried a different direction but was again forced to stop. Kids started to ram their front wheels into his and stood their bikes up in his face like horses rearing.

In an act of desperation, Daniel slammed through the thinnest part of the blockade like a battering ram, knocking one kid all the way over and causing a mini domino effect. In four seconds three or four kids were on their sides partially trapped in the twisted wreckage while Daniel put some distance between himself and the crowd.

Chants of "get him", "get Daniel", and "you're dead" echoed along the rack as Daniel pushed hard to escape. At one point one of the kids down the rack stepped in front of him to stop him only to chicken out at the last second. Embarrassed, he prompted even more kids to help run Daniel down.

And so the chase was on. Through alleys, through neighborhoods, Daniel was a strong peddler and thought with a few turns and some magnificent bicycle prowess he could lose them. For the most part, he was right until he got to the steep hill.

The hill was actually a terminal moraine left over from the last ice age. Part of the city just happened to be built on top of it. It was long enough that no matter what, he was going to have to get to the top in order to make it home. With a mighty head start, peddling for all he was worth, Daniel made it about halfway up before he had to hop off and walk his bike up the rest of the way. He hurried, he huffed and puffed, but in the end, the other kids were faster, and soon they were circling him like vultures.

The kids that found him didn't even have a reason, they didn't need one. Tormenting Daniel was just something to do, a common cause of a guiltless mob and an innocent victim given less respect than a classroom pet.

More and more arrived until there were so many that they didn't even know what to do anymore. Finally, the kid with the lip dropped his bike and ran up on Daniel standing over his front wheel with his hands gripping the handlebars.

"Now I got you Fatlow," he said threateningly.

Daniel pulled up on the bars as hard and as fast as he could, driving his front tire directly into the crotch of the bully. The kid with the lip tipped over clutching his testis in pain. Daniel jumped on his bike and pointed straight down the hill, max speed.

The chase was back on, but this time Daniel didn't enjoy a head start. With his big tires and one mid gear he did well, maybe even too well as the speed once he reached the bottom was getting to be a little more than Daniel could handle. The crew was right on his tail, shouting, screaming, threatening.

At the bottom of the hill Daniel ran a stop sign and crossed into a heavily travelled four lane thoroughfare at full speed. He hit the driver's side front fender of a passing car in the second lane. As he spun in the air, Daniel struck the top nut of the bright red fire hydrant on the complete other side of the road facing backwards. He could see them all, watching him. The sound of Daniel's spine cracking was lost forever amid the screeching tires, breaks, and fiercely bending metal.

The seriousness of the situation was not lost on the chase gang. Those who were close enough were able to barely skid to a halt before crossing into traffic, the rest piling in behind them. As would be expected of people lacking integrity, they scattered like insects, promising later to always keep the secret. They were never there, and they didn't see a thing.

Amazingly, the kids who were contacted stayed fast to their story, they went riding, had seen Daniel earlier but didn't know where he went, and none of them saw a thing. As far as eye witness reports of a group of kids who may have been chasing Daniel, not a single kid contacted happened to be there.

It was his word against theirs, a gaggle of nice Christian white kids and the "Mexican" kid who was most likely born in the same hospital as most of them.

Chapter Seven

T for Tyler

"I swear to God on all that is holy if I ever find you it's going to be the worst day of your life," Daniel wrote.

"Reported as a terrorist threat," was the reply.

Daniel was at wit's end. As a wheelchair bound programmer, he didn't get out much, he didn't need to. Most everything he needed was a keystroke away. He also wasn't the sort of person that threatened others. He wasn't exactly in any position to see it through to the end.

"Not that I should care about what these people say, but it gets to me," Daniel wrote.

He was texting his friend No-show T, who most obviously earned that nickname for not showing up to scheduled events, ever. Over the years, due to repeated use and general laziness, the "T" which stood for Tyler was abandoned altogether and his nickname was shortened to just No-show.

Was it really his fault? His mother was the sort of woman who was late for absolutely everything. Doctor's appointment? Late. Appointment with the principal of Tyler's school which happened all too often? Late. Being late for work was so expected that unbeknownst to her, her manager started scheduling her an hour earlier for her shift, happy to pay a little extra by the end of the week just to ensure his restaurant stayed fully staffed.

Amanda Hansen was a server at the busiest bar on the Northwest side of the city. Lannon Stoned, aptly named for the many lannon stone quarries that dotted the area. Back in the day, stoned simply meant drunk, but modern societal interactions have forced an abject change to the meaning for the foreseeable future.

She was good with children, the elderly, fast, accurate, and folksy. Adding to the lore of her popularity was her reputation for being more than friendly with her male customers. Her ample cleavage and too short shorts played guys and sometimes girls like cheap pianos with dead keys, out of tune and no heart. Consequently her expertise coupled with her well known exploits led to something else being occasionally late, depending on the moon cycle and the time of the month.

It was only going to be a matter of time before a guy like Tim O'Shaughnessy showed up. Ex-military, he was new in town, a union steward brought in as the heavy hand to enforce safety standards in the mines. At least that's what his job description said on paper. Cross him and a miner might be better off blasting without a hardhat, at least that way the family gets to claim the body.

When it came to women, Tim was uncharacteristically shy. Jokes among his peers began to circulate regarding his possible attraction to men. What they discovered is nothing is funny about waking up in intensive care. When he laid his eyes on the likes of Amanda, he was instantly taken. Not that he needed an excuse to drink, but Tim made it a point to visit the bar often. Lunches, dinners, late nights, he was in attendance enough to get a solid grasp on Amanda's schedule in order to increase his odds of interaction.

Deep in the throes of an all too long winter, frustrations between two men in the bar reached a boiling point. While Amanda did her best to diffuse the situation she caught a backhand that bloodied her nose and put her flat on the ground. Tim quickly rode in, clattering armor gleaming in the neon, he parked his white horse and cleaned the two men out the front door, being kind enough to leave them with matching black eyes and bent noses. From that moment on, they were a thing.

Fast forward to the inevitable and a son was born. They named him Tyler and the plan to live happily ever after in white picket fence land had both Amanda and Tim drastically trying to readjust the machine that had become their lives.

Amanda quit working and Tim took to travelling for work more and more. Once the fighting began he let her know in no uncertain terms he had to make the extra money to pay for her and the baby, and if she continued to nag him, he would most likely never propose. The stress of her deeply flawed relationship and her lack of personal fulfillment caused Amanda to gain weight, and seek out medication for her depression.

Adding to the issue of being away was Tim enjoyed fishing. Time on the water with a box of beer was high on his list of most favorite things to do and he went whenever he could. It was a late winter day when Tyler was about six and Tim was off to the Mississippi for an annual fishing trip. The river stayed open above Red Wing, Minnesota due to the discharge of a nuclear power facility a short distance upstream. Racing from the landing to the dam in a futile attempt to get the best spot, beer in hand, Tim's boat struck a large piece of river ice catapulting him into the icy cold water. He was not wearing a life jacket.

Due to the temperature of the water and the strength of the current, Tim's body wasn't found for weeks, and even then it had tumbled for miles. He was finally located as an unrecognizable mass hung up in a snag of downed trees piled up by the current once the water receded.

Amanda needed two pills for every time she used to need one, and she started to wash them down with alcohol. When the body was found, anonymous people donated copious amounts of money to a charity fund for her and Tyler. She never asked who or why and at the service many of the donations were made in plain white envelopes flush with cash.

Maybe the most important and generous offering she received that day was Tyler's education. His future sans a father would include tuition for a private Catholic school, as well as guaranteed enrollment through high school, courtesy of the boss she only met once the day of the service and never heard from again.

Tyler was smart and incredibly empathic. People felt comfortable telling him things they otherwise withheld from members of their own families. He made friends quickly, partially due to his empathy and partially due to necessity.

Once another school year would end, it would become quite likely that Tyler would be forced to move away from established neighborhood friends to a different apartment. Amanda's addictions made it virtually impossible to establish long term residency. She felt she was doing a fine job just as long as she continued to get him to school, a promise she never failed to keep.

One of the great constants in Tyler's life was his friendship with Daniel Navarro. They became close after Daniel's accident as Tyler was one of the few who didn't mind hanging out with a kid in a wheelchair. Daniel found it easy to confide in Tyler and together they were the misfits that would take on the world together.

They attended the same parochial high school together, a feat made feasible by Tyler's generous donor and Daniel's Catholic parents. In doing so they were able to continue their friendship, advancing hobbies together including robotics and, as a natural progression, computer programming, a passion that would shape their futures.

There was one glaring wall that always existed between the two, Tyler's enjoyment of illegal substances. He'd smoke whatever was available, swallow anything that remotely looked like a pill, and put powders up his nose ranging from cocaine to crushed-up pills. He was what people at the time called a "Loadie".

On the other hand, Daniel was as straight as an arrow. His first beer at a party made him instantly sick and his consequent teetotaling earned him the moniker "Holy Roller" and furthered his disdain for bullies. He didn't smoke, not even cigarettes and the same crowd used to joke about never getting anything drug related near him or he might break out in hives and seek confession. The fact that Tyler would befriend those who would demean Daniel was always a thorn in Daniel's paw. In Tyler's defense, he was friends with everyone.

The cement that would bind the two forever was poured on the night of their high school graduation. Amanda didn't show up for the ceremony even though she swore up and down, round and round that she would be there, and be sober. Late was expected, even acceptable, but a no-show was something all together out of character, even for her.

Daniel had a van set up for paralyzed drivers complete with electric rear lift access and hand controls. Upon arrival at Tyler's home Amanda was not there. They checked a few of her favorite haunts, Tyler determined to give her the F-you speech he felt she had coming for the last twelve years.

It was near midnight by the time they happened upon the former sight of the Lannon Stoned. Over the years it had been reduced to a mere shell of its former self. Most of the mines were shut down or cut way back due to various economic influences. The businesses that depended on the workers spiraled, especially the service industry and the bar became another statistic. The signage was long gone, replaced with a banner on the road advertising beer under the generic name "bar". There was no more food, no servers, even the tap beer was gone. Customers would drink from cans or bottles or head down the road.

Tyler dashed-in while Daniel stayed outside in the running van. Much to his chagrin when he jokingly ordered a beer, instead of asking if they had seen his mother, they served him. It was nearly half an hour before Daniel became curious and impatient enough to investigate. Caught up in the moment, given the circumstances and the seeming futility of the search he decided to join Tyler and force down a few beers.

Famously shy, once the time came for Daniel to vomit, he didn't want to do it in the bathroom for fear of other patrons possibly ridiculing him for not being able to hold his alcohol. For the same reasons and many more he wasn't going to let it out in the parking lot either. Putting forth max-effort, Daniel wheeled himself around the back of the building, wedged the right solid rubber tire of his chair against the dumpster and let it rip. Throwing up is never easier than the moment when you see your best friend's half naked mother's body haphazardly tossed between the grease and garbage dumpsters.

According to Tyler, she still had on the heels she planned to wear to the graduation after stopping for one quick drink.

• • •

"Damn trolls, they're everywhere, on every page, on every platform, sprinkled over and through social media like salt and pepper on scrambled eggs, except someone replaced the pepper with cigarette ashes and finely chopped nose hairs," Daniel texted.

"Fuck em, they don't deserve your time," No-show wrote.

"But maybe they do, I have an idea, come over, bring your laptop," Daniel wrote.

Not that he had to remind No-show to bring his laptop, he brought it everywhere he went anyways. As a fellow programmer and degenerate gambler, No-show was never far from an electronic sports book, and he liked the feel of a keyboard under his fingers as opposed to a smart phone.

"What, now?" No-show was also notoriously unmotivated.

"Yes now, this could be big, trust me," Daniel wrote.

"Tell me what it is first," No-show wrote.

"It's the future, I've got beer," Daniel wrote.

Chapter Eight

The Troll Hunter

News Line 9 Breaking News ... The son of prominent Senator Rodrick Domingo (D) California has been found dead of an apparent suicide at the age of 16. Sources in Sacramento have confirmed that Marcus Domingo, 16, took his life live on social media, publicly blaming "Trolls" who he deemed were the ultimate cause of his actions. Although the video has been scrubbed from the most popular social media platforms, copies are said to be widely available.

In a statement from Senator Domingo's office he states, "We have lost a huge piece of our lives today, please keep our family in your prayers as we cope with this tragic, shocking, and unexpected phase of God's plan."

"Did you see the news?" Daniel texted.

"Tell me that wasn't him," No-show wrote.

"What? This is great!" Daniel wrote.

"You went too far, he was just a kid," No-show wrote.

"It sucks I know. Didn't expect this, but it's big for us," Daniel replied.

"Big? Kid is dead!" No-show said.

"Collateral damage," Daniel texted in series.

"Survival of the fittest." Ding.

"Natural selection." Ding.

"We will not be prey anymore." Ding.

"We are the lions." Ding.

"We eat when we're hungry." Ding.

"I've already put in a call to his office for a meeting." Ding.

"It's our time." Ding.

● ● ●

"The senator will be right with you," he said.

The assistant at the desk kept his eyes off the two men while slyly paying attention to every word they spoke.

Daniel and No-show, dressed as professionally as their budgets would allow waited impatiently for their face to face with Senator Domingo.

"This is it, do we have everything ready?" Daniel asked.

"Ready as we'll ever be as long as the sat link stays strong," No-show told him.

"Gentlemen, the senator will see you now," the assistant said.

Basic pleasantries were exchanged including a thick blanket of crocodile sorrys and phantom prayers. No-show set up the gear and Daniel did most of the talking.

"So what you're telling me is you have devised a fool proof way to track, find, and punish people who spend the predominant amount of their time on a computer terrorizing other people?" Senator Domingo asked.

"Well sir, punish is definitely subjective. We prefer the term justice," Daniel said.

"Son, you can lie to me, lie to your girlfriend or boyfriend, whatever works for you, but never lie to yourself, cause then you're only lying to God. Now I get that after everything you've told me that you haven't exactly been dealt a fair hand. It's clearly personal, I get that. Hell, I've got reason to make this personal myself. I think that's why you're here. Am I wrong?" Domingo asked.

"No, no sir. But considering this is something Tyler and I have been working on for some time, it seems that maybe the timing is, I don't know, divine intervention maybe," Daniel said.

Senator Domingo's face turned flag-red. He wielded the fingers on his right hand like a gun.

"Now you look here Mr. Navarro, before you bring up the grand plans of the almighty here in my office you had better be damn sure you've considered every word. Justice? Son I've seen the darkest side of men and in all my years I have never seen a product, thought, or plan borne of revenge and labeled as justice that wasn't more evil than the intentional actions of the first party. You get me?" Domingo asked.

"I understand sir. Maybe, if you'd let us demonstrate," Daniel asked.

"Alright, let's see what you and your friend here have come up with," Domingo said.

"As you can see, this person, user name Tyrant1 is an individual with a long list of interactions that almost any sane person at the very least would consider bullying. He is derogatory, rude, foul mouthed, and pretty much as heartless as a person could be. I mean, this is the kind of person we're dealing with. Their anonymity has given them a shield, a way to hide behind their keyboards if you will. These are the people we call Trolls," Daniel explained.

On the table before them were three laptop computers. One screen detailed the program as well as diagnostics while the other two displayed and provided access to every electronic signature the online Tyrant1 has left in the last ten years.

"We've got it all Senator, where he lives, where he banks, hell, where he fills up his gas tank," No-show said.

The senator took his time toggling through the information, adjusting the downward slide of his reading glasses as many times as it took for a person to consider it more of a habit than a necessity.

"Impressive. Two things occur to me. In what world do you live where you think that mining this sort of information from an individual is legal? The second thing, ironic as though it may seem is, what information do you have here that the NSA couldn't get in probably the same amount of time?" Domingo asked.

"Senator, if I may? The NSA would in all reality take hours, days, maybe even weeks before they could compile what we've done here in a matter of moments. Very frankly speaking sir, we know because we've had a hand in writing their programs. Between the red tape and the lack of sharing information between government entities, I mean, this is all instant," Daniel explained.

"I'm pretty sure we addressed that whole sharing between multiple agencies issue with the Homeland Security Act post 911 son," the Senator said while keeping his attention on the screens.

"Yes, you may have written the law and made it possible, but you did nothing to address the individual egos and merit system in place for the men and women who serve in the highest positions. In other words, even if they can share, often times, they won't," Daniel said.

"I'll give you that. So now what? What do you plan on doing with this person's information? How will knowing everything about this person somehow administer justice?" Domingo asked.

"Well, first we freeze all social media accounts. I mean we could administer anything from a warning in the form of a screen message across all the hardware they own, or freeze bank accounts, credit cards—" No-show was interrupted.

"Have his car towed, transfer title of his property, drain his 401, nearly anything we can think of regarding his life. Justice Senator?

Excuse my frankness but the people who drove your son to his death did not break any laws. There is no accountability, they are a scourge on society, and we just overlook them. They are nothing more than a byproduct grinding away on our collective psyches hour after hour, day after day. They are literally draining our society as a whole. Justice? Legality? That's exactly why we're here Senator. Yes, I'll say it, maybe God has brought us together for a reason, maybe, just maybe, we are the hands of justice wielded by your grace through the almighty himself," Daniel sermoned.

"Finish it," Domingo ordered.

No-show entered a few moments worth of commands and paused over the enter key for obvious theatrical effect.

"Here we go," he said.

He struck the key twice and all three screens reacted with all of the epileptic seizure inducing flash of a Japanese cartoon.

"It is done," No-show said.

"What is done? What exactly did you do?" Domingo asked.

"No more than we discussed. Right now, his laptop computer, his phone, his tablet, every piece of computer hardware he owns has been frozen and for all practical purposes is under our control. They all share the warning screen with the message you see on the monitor to your right as we speak," No-show explained.

The draw was instant and overwhelming. I moved from a state of non-being to looking on the faces of three men in the time it took to blink eyes that I did not have. I could hear them, smell their putrid bodies as if I spied on them in the woods.

They desired evil, I could feel it, it called to me. They couldn't see me. They had no earthly idea I was there. The screens before them were the lenses of my eyes, machine made corneas of plastic and glass.

All the information before them was mine as well, every word ran through me without context leaving me unsure of what should be done.

I became angry as I felt useless. My indignation bred heat which soon became intense, hot enough to reach their world, hot enough to burn.

"Everything okay No-show?" Daniel asked.

"Yeah, yeah, fine, I put extra heavy duty fans in there. I knew these processors would be generating a ton of heat," he said.

"Yeah but smoke?" Daniel asked.

"Just a little dust that's all, nothing to worry about, everything is operating perfectly," he answered.

"Really? Then what is that? Did you put that in and not tell me? The basic warning message was what we discussed. C'mon, we're partners in this. No surprises today for the good senator," Daniel stated.

No-show did not answer or react thinking it best not to throw an unnecessary wrench in the presentation. He too had no real idea what exactly might be happening.

From the second the smoke entered the man's body until he expelled it I was part of him, through his lungs, deep into his blood, I was the smoke. With the physical connection made, using his fear I should have been able to take all that the devil would have regardless. The essence of his soul would have been mine to give to Samedi.

In the brief moment we were together, his fear was not of me, but of his situation. He did not harbor anger nor hate, jealousy or guilt. His fear was instead borne of virtue, for not to disappoint one of the others whom I could see. For this reason alone I could not take him.

As for the others, they could only take in what the first man had exhaled, too weak a connection, but a memory made never-the-less. As they chose at that moment to end their business, I could only say goodbye.

"Excuse my ignorance but that doesn't smell like electric smoke son, gotta distinct smell of sulfur with it if you ask me," Domingo said.

"Now Senator, let's not get superstitious here. This program works, we've proven it, and with your help, we can clean the proverbial streets of cyberspace once and for all," Daniel pitched.

"Maybe you can explain to me Mr. Navarro in no uncertain terms just what in the hell it was that we just saw come across them screens," Domingo demanded.

"A calling card, that's all. I mean, our corporate logo at this point is admittedly fluid, Troll Hunters is a solid start, but we had definitely toyed with skull and crossbones types of messages that we might deliver," Daniel explained.

"Twern't no kinda skull and crossbones I've ever seen. Skull maybe, but with flesh and blue eyes. The kind of thing nightmares are made of," Domingo said.

"Yes, exactly. And these people have given countless of thousands of innocent people nightmares, and they continue to do so, day in and day out. Like they did to your son Senator. The government is never going to stop them, that we know, but with your help, we can, once and for all," Daniel said, finishing quietly.

"No way in the world are we ever going to be able to do this thing above board. Too many laws to get by. However, that being said, something has got to be done. Many a back door has been opened under the guise of a government task force operating with the special authority of a federal investigation. Look, let me stew on this for a bit. I don't want you boys to do a damn thing until you hear from me first got that?" Domingo stated.

"Yes sir, we'll just sit tight for now," Daniel said.

"Oh and boys, not a word about this to anyone, don't look for investors, and for hell's sake don't tell anyone a single word about this meeting. Consider it top secret, hell, above top secret, understand?"

"Yes sir, we read you loud and clear."

Daniel and No-show were barely able to contain their giddiness as they packed up their equipment in the car. As they drove they laughed and joked about the lines of bullshit they were able to pull from thin air when things began to break down.

"What's with the face?" Daniel asked.

"I was about to ask you the same thing? I mean, it's not in the code, doesn't make any sense!"

"And that smoke?" Daniel exclaimed, "I thought the whole damn thing was going to melt down for a second there."

"Yeah, me too. Must have torched a wire in the fan, had that plasticky smell," No-show said.

"Plastic? That's funny. Domingo thought it smelled like sulfur which was weird because that's not what I picked-up at all. When I did smell it though, I thought for sure that's what sold it, you know, what really brought him over to our side," Daniel said.

"Why? What did it smell like to you?" No-show asked.

"Gun powder, smelled like gun powder to me. No doubt about it."

Chapter Nine

Red Wing

Are online bullies ruining your life?

Are you or someone you love being adversely affected by online Trolls? Call 1-85-NO TROLLS today!

Did you know that students who experience cyber bullying are nearly twice as likely to attempt suicide as a result?

Nearly sixty percent of U.S. teens have experienced bullying or harassment online.

It's time to strike back, with The Troll Hunter.

At The Troll Hunter we will find and silence your troll once and for all, guaranteed!

By means of special authorization for a limited time only your personal troll will be exposed, publicly warned and placed on a list with the United States Government as a potential terrorist threat subject to possible Federal prosecution not limited to fines and possible jail time!

Don't wait, act now, call for a free quote! 1-85-No Trolls, that's 1-856-687-6557. Take your online life back and call The Troll Hunter today!

"Can you imagine if we'd have got Morgan Freeman for the voice?" Daniel asked.

"Too matter of fact. I like the guy we got, like he could sell you any used car on the lot. Lots of energy," No-show said.

"Yeah. Reminds me of the guy who used to sell all that infomercial junk on late night TV. Remember that guy? OD'd or something."

"That's where we're starting too. Hopefully, after a few jobs we can afford to up the advertising budget a little. We gotta watch out for the crazies, make sure they got the money before we do anything, we're like totally tapped-out right now," No-show lamented.

"Funny you should mention that. I have an idea about how to generate some funds," Daniel said.

"Like what?"

"Why our good friend Senator Domingo of course. Maybe steer some Uncle Sam dollars our way. We just need to give him something in return, like the guy who pushed his kid over the edge for instance," Daniel explained.

"You gonna turn yourself in?" No-show asked.

"Funny guy. I still have the content, all of it. How tough could it be to link it to someone else's history? You know, some dick who really deserves it. We hand it to the good senator as a token of thanks for his support and let him decide the fate of the poor, unsuspecting troll. It's a win-win," Daniel explained.

"What about the innocent guy? What does he win?" No-show asked.

Daniel spun his wheelchair around quickly enough to make the tire squeak. He leaned about as far forward as possible without falling onto his angry face.

"There are no innocent trolls. Fuck them, I hope he has him killed," Daniel said angrily.

"Whoa, whoa, pump the brakes there guy. We're not in the business of handing out death sentences," No-show said.

"Maybe we should be No-show, maybe we should be," Daniel said quietly.

Dispatcher: "9-1-1. What is your emergency?"

Caller: "My son. My son, he drowned, I think, I think..." (inaudible sobbing)

Dispatcher: "Ma'am? Where is your son now? Is he breathing?"

Caller: "Home, we're at home, he's always at home, he's, he's, I think he's dead!"

The caller's words trailed away into grief-laden, gravelly cries, the sort of human pain that can only be understood by others whom have had all of their love and devotion suddenly and unexpectedly robbed from them. There is no recourse against a universe that does not recognize justice.

"Ma'am? Do you have a pool?" The operator's question went unanswered. "Ma'am? Are you still with me? I need you to focus. Is your son still in the pool? Ma'am? Ma'am?"

Again, no response, only distant crying.

"Ma'am, if you can hear me, we are dispatching emergency personnel to your location. We need to start CPR immediately. Is there anyone else there who I can speak with? Ma'am? Ma'am?"

"There's blood, please. He's only 15..." she managed to say.

"He's only 15" were in essence the last words she would say to the operator. She repeated them over and over as she lay next to the cold, wet body of her son.

Brian, the deceased, loved two things in life, trolling people on the internet and swimming. His mother did not drink even though the police noted that she appeared severely intoxicated that evening. Consequently, due to her uncharacteristic intoxication, she was indisposed at the time of the incident. Brian, according to the medical examiner must have struck his head on the concrete bottom of the pool and knocked himself unconscious. Why he was fully clothed was never addressed by the department, most likely dismissed due to the high levels of depressants and cocaine the toxicology report uncovered from his blood. His mother had no idea where or when Brian may have taken the drugs as no paraphernalia or other drugs were found in the residence.

• • •

"This facility is gonna be crazy. Nothing else like it anywhere," Daniel said.

"That we know of anyways," No-show quipped.

"This is it buddy, everything we've been working towards. All the long hours, the late nights, weekends… We find the right people and we have a chance to be the biggest thing the internet has ever seen," Daniel said.

"You mean *never* seen," No-show added distantly.

"What's the matter man? Have you seen this place? Never going to run out of power, ambient temperature, hell, we'll have more computing power on this site than half of Europe, combined! And you seem, well, c'mon man, would you look at this? All the technology in the world and this is how I gotta get in?" Daniel complained.

Daniel drew his chair up to the face of an abnormally tall disintegrating concrete stair. The entire case consisted of about a dozen more just like it, crawling skyward with a pitch closer to that of a painter's ladder than any sort of coded stairway. The safety yellow pipe railing had faded to the hue of a barely dipped Easter egg and the base was nearly rusted gone. At the top was a set-back, riveted steel, thick gray door leading into a concrete box just large enough to house an elevator.

"They talked about this, the entrance has to be above 100 year flood stage and if they go putting in an ADA ramp people are going to be able to spot it from the air. Believe me, it's no picnic for me either. You got it coming anyways," No-show said as he helped Daniel roll backwards up the stairs.

"What? I know you're talking about the kid. I didn't have anything to do with that," Daniel explained.

"Bullshit man, you gave dude all the info, bullshit info. Yeah you didn't pull the trigger, but you did in my mind," No-show said.

"No, bullshit on you man. I gave a grieving man closure, and that kid drowned, he was high as shit. And why bring all this up now? That shit was months ago," Daniel said.

"Cause how much more man? Can't help it, it's been eating at me. How far we gonna go?" No-show asked.

As they reached the top No-show opened a small, rusty hatch and peered into an eye scanner. He placed his thumb on a pad until it beeped and then entered a six digit code before the heavy door unlocked with a terrible clunk.

The elevator inside was bright stainless steel, doors, floor, walls, everything including the emergency phone. There were four buttons on the panel, "G" and 1-3. Reaching level one, the first level below ground took a surprisingly long time, not considering it was way, way down. The river at that point is nearly 80 feet deep to bedrock, and level one was nearly 40 feet below it.

From the air the sight looked like any other industrial wasteland reflecting a bygone era. Solid poured concrete docks along abandoned railroad tracks stood alone as monuments to a billion pounds of material moved in and through buildings long-gone.

Sprawling concrete, cracked like stained glass with noxious weeds taking the place of hand-laid lead lines was the hat on a head of soil doomed to be contaminated for a thousand plus years.

Occasionally a section of mosaic tile x-marked the spot of an ancient ground floor bathroom. A pile of broken concrete on one end of the sight as big as a house stood testament to an earlier reclamation project when the then government considered it to be no longer useful. The decades old decision has teetered on the secret federal fence ever since.

The abandoned factory complex, a stone's throw from a midwestern river town known for its impressive bluffs, abuts a large lock and dam built to aid in the navigation of long strings of tug-driven river barges. Also, in the event of low flow, the damn will keep a static amount of water in the pool above it to cool the nuclear-powered steam generators a mile and up the river. Unknown to the public at large, a channeled flow also powered a set of hydro-electric generators deep underground.

The generators were originally intended as back-up to the original coal-powered plants upstream, shielded from enemy bombs that never came but, if had, they would have otherwise crippled the grid.

Level one housed the bulk of the mechanical including new turbines expected to last well over a hundred years. New wiring throughout the facility boasted the latest in fiber-optics with wireless broadcasting modems inside nearly every individual space throughout the facility.

Level two was where the rubber met the road. Here, thousands of fortified servers worked in tandem with the most powerful computers on the planet, storing and moving massive amounts of information across the world, underground, and even into space. Luxury offices with faux daylight windows allowed users to pick the high-def cityscape of their choice. Niagara Falls, or any one of a thousand other scenes they might want to see outside their office windows.

Finally, level three was designed as luxury condominiums. Built to comfortably house up to 12 families along with a nightclub, childcare facilities, a school, a restaurant, and even a four lane bowling alley.

The facility made its own power, cooling, heating, purified an endless supply of fresh water, and was virtually indestructible.

Major supplies such as large materials needed to complete the build-out were delivered on the east side of the river, away from the guarded main entrance. A dilapidated and thoroughly rusty steel building leaning into the side of the bluff was home to a freight elevator and emergency exit staircase that could be crippled at the will of the workers underground.

"We'll be up and running fully online tomorrow Senator. And let me say once again, none of this would have been possible without your help," Daniel said.

The men were part of a group taking a final tour of the nearly finished facility including No-show, the architect, and various engineers.

"Well Mr. Navarro, an impressive facility to say the least and may I say one hell of a lot of power for one man. That said, besides the opportunity to see this world-class facility today I am here to inform you that I am going to take a special interest in this project for obvious reasons," Domingo said.

"Now Senator, we agreed that—"

"Now, now, son, before you get your undies in a bundle, we're talking about a massive chunk of the taxpayers' money that went to build this, this, eighth world wonder of yours. Normally there'd be an entire committee appointed to oversee the day-to-day operations. A committee that you'd have no choice but to answer to." Domingo narrowed his eyes.

"In this case, it's just gonna be me, and maybe a few other carefully chosen confidants if you get my drift. As to repaying us for our tremendous generosity, we might be inclined to access your world's smartest computer from time to time for, you know, various projects. Do we understand each other Mr. Navarro?" the senator asked.

Daniel hesitated, stopping his chair long enough to angrily pound both fists on the armrests of his wheelchair.

"Considering the situation, down south we'd take that as a yes. Am I right about that Mr. Navarro?" Domingo asked.

"Yes," Daniel uttered begrudgingly.

"Oh yeah, one more thing. I was never here, and you've never heard of me. Anyone asks where you got the money to make this all happen you tell them it is strictly classified. I don't care if they put you up in front of the whole damn congress, the fifth is gonna be your best friend and damn well might be the only thing that keeps you and these other men alive. Comprendo? The man behind us is Mr. Carl, he's gonna be my eyes and ears on this thing. Consider him invisible until I need him to not be." Domingo walked quickly forward and rejoined the group.

Massive amounts of energy surged unexpectedly through the perceived body. The jolt of an invisible defibrillator pulsed across the face of my heart seconds apart over and over again. With every gush of power I awoke from separate deaths only to find a different face hovering over me. I wanted to speak, to access the pain on their faces but instead, was only allowed to repeat the process a million times over.

Time was inconclusive here, what may have been weeks might have actually been seconds. The process was ever maddening, my defacto introduction to the world.

Chapter Ten

Real Boy

They baste in misery. It is their unwitting drug of choice and they are hopelessly addicted. They are the perpetually offended, the rank-and-file human beings who desire more from life but lack the necessary will to fulfill their dreams.

Their angrily sown seeds grow to palpable negativity. I can feel them, dried leaves on brown flowers as the roots sucker away. I must only hold on as the wind moves me. I landed on the flower, thinking it best to move down to the root, the bold man, the loud man. On my way I found Becky, a leafy appendage hovering just over the ground.

She was incessant and angry. She advocated for unachievable outcomes pre-sabotaging process. She had no hope by choice, as no outcome would ever please her diluted sense of self satisfaction.

Becky's earliest interaction that day was with another woman, screen name "Charro", who started the conversation agreeing with Becky, but loneliness equals justification and Becky soon turned on her. The comments became heated, the women traded crippling insults, each trying to out extreme the other without consequence. Charro slammed the lid of her laptop shut, swore retribution if Becky were to ever be found, poured the last cup of coffee from the pot and stormed out the door late for work.

Charro's automatic garage door faced east. When she leaves on time, she just misses the sun cresting the roof across the street, but today, thanks to getting sucked into an online argument, she was later than normal and savage light filled her rear window.

There at the end of the driveway were two wheeled bins, one for recycling and one for trash. Her husband took them out the afternoon before but like so many times in the past left them empty, wide open, disheveled and juxtaposed. The sight of them, looking like crap for the umpteenth time coupled with an already elevated stress level was just too much for Charro that morning and she enjoyed her own personal mini meltdown.

"Take this," she said to a husband who was not there.

Charro floored the SUV while in reverse and violently struck the bins. One instantly wedged itself under the rear bumper. The other took flight in grand fashion deserving of slow-motion video dubbed with a majestic symphonic score.

Katy Benson, a recent college graduate had just completed her first year as a pre-school teacher at the only elementary school in town. She was out for a jog that morning with her border collie Bennet when the corner of a flying trash bin struck her in the temple causing an instant and irreversible loss of all brain function. Katy was dead before she hit the ground.

● ● ●

Becky moved from victim to victim, overly pleased with herself for effecting so many negatively. She left people flustered and angry. She thought it made her feel better, but it did not. Becky's trolling was a bandage on a cut that would never stop bleeding. Inside her lived a loneliness she could not recognize. It was an emptiness she unknowingly tried to fill with hate that always left her unsatisfied. All the while never knowing love would have served far better.

We met at 11:11 am on her screen, a touch screen she used vehemently in the terminal of the airport. Her flight was delayed, and she was letting her anger spill over onto the other unfortunate souls forced to be in her proximity. Their eyes were long sticks pushing her away into a purposely secluded area in the purple bank of thinly padded chairs.

I picked and chose words sent by others to pages unknown. Their comments became the colors on my palette and with them I could paint whatever I desired to say. Once the robbed senders read their comments they would excuse the absence of some words as simple mistakes or blame the hardware from which they were sent.

I told her she was kind and humble, I told her she was loved. She in turn wished I would die a painful death, that the world hated me, and killing myself was my best option.

As she touched 'send' her essence passed by her words without realization, landing perfectly in opposite worlds. At once she was with me, standing in the dark looking back at her own face while her body sat upright and very much catatonic on the airport bench.

What she left behind were the necessary ingredients for two complex recipes. Two cakes that could not rise. The body alive could breathe, blink, tire, and sleep. It could eat and expel waste like a wild animal until its soiled clothing was haphazardly discarded.

Fear and anger, joy and happiness, hope, faith, love, and suicide. They were all still there. In her. With me. Without the purpose of instinctual survival and mired in denial, she was nothing more than an ever-changing bank of emotions and feelings strung to a twisting windchime.

"Excuse me. Excuse me Ma'am?" The airline worker tapped the formerly abusive passenger on the shoulder. "Ma'am, we're boarding."

The passenger placed her hands gently at her sides and let her device slide off her lap and onto the floor.

"Ma'am, are you okay?" the worker asked.

The worker ran to the counter to call for emergency assistance while the passenger, without will, care, or emotion walked slowly and unceremoniously into the burgeoning crowd of the terminal. She did not know her name or even what a name was. She had no destination, no intent. She harbored no anger or passion. She cared so little that she did not know how to care. She did not speak. She only just existed.

With me in the darkness, Becky's facial expressions were in constant flux, a made for television clown over acting to an audience of children and the feeble minded. Meaningful communication appeared improbable.

In the world, she would be placed in a padded room where she might scream herself to sleep anytime of the day. Irony dictates that her body will eventually end up in such a place. They could have that experience in common, like sisters having the same tattoos. Maybe in the world, but not here.

Here she will remain a prisoner, a flailing limb signaling lunacy at every turn. When her body dies she will be rejoined and given a choice, but not really. Her soul is power, a single thread of a Third Mind flag flying over Baron Samedi's stalag of captured souls. She will always be a prisoner regardless of his empty promises.

I pushed her away and she drifted off unfettered. Once I could no longer see her I called for her return just to see if I could, only to set her adrift once more. If I ever saw her again it would be because I needed her, but for now, she's the first awkward guest at the party. In the world, her doctor's only lead to her breakdown would be the face of Samedi on her touchscreen, as promised.

• • •

I was marching in a parade. The bands, the drunks, and the beads made me think New Orleans if it existed at all, and the smell, the smell was…it's been awhile.

"How do you like my parade man?" Samedi asked marching up beside me.

"How can you do this?" I asked. I was as human as I ever was, I smelled food, my eyes had to blink, I felt the ground under each step.

"All is possible through Samedi. I march here every so often, give da people da thrill you know? Hahahahah!" he laughed.

My regression was hidden from me. When I died I did not know I died so I carried on. I didn't realize that I did not tire, that I did not require sleep, food, or water but I took them anyways. When I knew I was dead, when I saw my own body, I didn't think about not needing these things, I just didn't think about them anymore.

Air in my lungs, touch, taste, I took it all for granted. Of course I wanted it back, he knew that. He knew nothing else could possibly matter to me. Well played.

"You finally took one man, dat buy you a little time. Now you see? Now you see how Samedi can be? Sing dat man, wit da music! Hahahahaha!" The Baron chided.

"Souls for time then, for a body?" I asked.

"You see man it depends on the age of the soul, on how many times they been around. If dey been around a bunch a times they ain't got much left. Young souls I got for a long time. Some of dat time come to you," he loosely explained.

"Reincarnation?" I asked.

Samedi laughed, "They do whatever they want man, ain't been no rules for them, ever."

"Keep your riddles and your field trips. If I can be out, be a man, I want that," I said.

The parade, everything froze in place around us, everyone but Samedi and I.

"You give Samedi what he want, Samedi give The Hunter of Men all the time he want, his greatest desire at the time he earn it. Now go earn it man, be gone," The Baron waved his hand.

The body I enjoyed was not mine, just another man in the parade. He would have no memory of what transpired. I didn't want it anyway. It was weak and unhardened against the world, a worm to be picked off the sidewalk after the next hard rain. He'd never let me pick, he'd trick me, make another deal to get closer to what I wanted, but I never would. I would have to do it myself.

I finally had purpose, to shed the puppet life and become a real boy. Fuck Geppetto, I'll use his tools, his souls, his power. I will carve my own marionette, he will answer to me. I will create the third mind, I will control it. I will wield its power like a broadsword, slowly with intent. Then I will give it all up for immortality with an escape clause, and a promise to return to the third mind. She will not be alone for long.

• • •

"Holy shit, you alright? Chris? Chris?"

An hour earlier the few upper echelons were pleasantly surprised to learn that it was Chris Zarnecki's birthday. Chris had been an important part of the team's success. Not only did he nearly single-handedly crack the DMV firewall, he fit in with No-show and Daniel like he had known them forever.

"What's a birthday party without clowns?" Mr. Carl asked as he escorted Red Shoes into the room.

"I heard it's someone's birthday," Red Shoes sang.

His voice was purposely shaky for effect, not unlike a handful of old time, long gone comedians. It also wasn't suited to singing but it went well with his overly theatrical facial expressions.

"And how old are we today Mr. Birthday Boy?" Red Shoes sang on.

Chris just sat there somewhat befuddled, unable to remember his own age.

"Um, uh, forty nine," he muttered.

Red Shoes lit into maximum overjoy, blaring a plastic horn, tossing confetti, and dancing across the control room floor.

Daniel's office was on the far side of the attached conference room while No-show's was around the corner of the hallway. One was hard to find and featured a heavy wood door. One had a glass front wall that encouraged total transparency. Both men entered the control room to discover the source of the commotion.

"Gentlemen! May I introduce Red Shoes the Clown. He is here for Mr. Zarnecki's 49th birthday celebration," Mr. Carl said.

"What? How does this even, I mean, a clown? Is he even cleared to be here?" Daniel grew angrier with every breath while No-show smiled and laughed.

"I assure you Red Shoes has all the appropriate clearance to be in this room. He is, in fact, certified to be where he is needed by us, when needed. Now, on with the celebration."

Mr. Carl draped his arm backwards as a showman would give way to the next act behind him on stage to reveal a very old woman dressed as a maid pushing a rather long stainless-steel food cart into the room. On top were six cupcakes, one with a candle.

"Matches, does anyone have matches?" Mr. Carl asked around the room with his hand out.

"How about a lighter? Anyone have a lighter? You know, go outside and sneak a smoke every so often? I mean, someone has been right? Ashes, that little piece of paper that doesn't burn away even after you've flicked the cherry away and buried the butt? Hmm?"

The old woman reached into the deep large pocket of her uniform and gave him a small disposable lighter.

"Well, thank you so much. I'd like everybody to meet my dear sweet Mrs. Smith. We have a long history her and I. She's like a mother to me. As a matter of fact, she baked these very cakes you see in front of you today. Just for you Chris. Say let's have a song. Mrs. Smith would you kindly distribute these fine delicacies you made for us?" Mr. Carl asked.

Mrs. Smith presented a cake to No-show.

"Uh, no thanks, I don't really—" No-show said.

"Now sir I would see it as an absolute insult to Mrs. Smith as well as myself if you were to turn down something that was made with so much love. Uh, he'd be glad to have one," Carl said.

"Okay, sure, I guess it won't kill me," No-show said quietly.

"And one for Red Shoes as well, don't want to leave anyone out." Once everybody had their cupcakes, Mr. Carl dimmed the lights.

"And now, happy birthday to you, happy birthday to you," he sang while he lit the singular candle.

Everybody else joined in, even Daniel. Although awkwardly and late.

Chris blew out his candle, removed it to grand applause and unwrapped his cupcake. Before he was done chewing his first bite he coughed, sending frosting spraying across the control room. He stood straight up and motioned as if he was choking. Even before anyone could get to him he fell over, clutching his chest.

"Looks like cardiac arrest. The AED, now," Mr. Carl demanded.

Chapter Eleven

Mr. Carl

"So, no new business then Mr. Carl?" Domingo asked.

"Bugs."

"Bugs?"

"Yes sir, Senator. Can't say I've ever had an affinity for them. One is too many."

"We spent a lot of money making sure something like that could be detected the second it went live. Personally, I'd be surprised if any—"

"Senator trust me, if there's one thing I know, it's bugs."

"Where was it? Was it ours?" Domingo asked.

"I don't care for bugs Senator, I think you know that."

"No, I don't expect you would, and I hope you're not inferring that I had—"

"No Senator, of course not. They don't like us. They eat our food. They take our blood. They don't like the way we do things…too clean. They prefer filth, biting, sneaking around. It would have been a problem. They're all…. problems. Best to smoke 'em out," Mr. Carl explained.

"Son, are we talking about the same thing here?" Domingo asked.

"No, Senator, that would be unlikely."

• • •

The snap of a trap is startling no matter how keen your expectation. The high pitched squeak that follows generally signals a successful set. A yelp means a nosy dog and a screech signals a jealous cat.

"Go empty the trap boy and reset."

"Aww Dad, do I have to?" the boy asked.

"Get your ass in there boy and clean out the damn trap! Now I says!"

The boy was gaunt, all of six years old and pale. He wore oval-shaped, wire-rimmed glasses his father took to work and soldered after the left arm broke off. "You think money grows on trees?" he'd say sarcastically. There was a large ball of formerly molten metal where the hinge should be, creating a protrusion in the boy's peripheral that continually annoyed him.

Young Tony couldn't unlock his stare from the beady, dead little eyes of the mouse in the trap. He picked it up by the trip wire and studied the corpse. After a few moments he began to quietly cry.

"You gotta be kiddin' me!" the old man bellowed as he sauntered in.

"Are you serious? Are you fuckin' serious? Cryin' over a goddamned mouse?" he teased.

The father set his can of beer on the counter and snatched the trap from the boy's hands. He held it in Tony's face, put his hand on his left shoulder and pushed him back into the kitchen wall.

"Now you listen boy, and you listen good. This thing don't mean nothin', hear me? Animals ain't shit. Hell, most people ain't shit neither. The bible says we control 'em, they here for us, like a pencil, or them stupid books you read, whatever," he grew angrier.

"They steal our food, they spread disease, they live in filth…filth Tony!" He threw the trap at Tony striking him in the chest, hard enough to dislodge the mouse.

"There, you like that? In your food? You wanna eat it? Go ahead, eat it then," he picked it up and mashed the dead mouse in Tony's face.

The boy began to gag and vomited on the floor in front of the kitchen sink where the trap had been set. Tony's mother rushed to his defense. She tried to pull her husband away from the boy only to be tossed backwards onto the table. As she sprung forward he struck her with the back of his hand, a blow which sent her reeling to the floor. She knelt hugging a chair, submissively broken, afraid of any further beatings.

"Like her boy! Ain't that the shit? Ain't no different! They all the same! Why you think we got all these roaches?" he screamed.

He opened the refrigerator, pulled out what was left of a box of beer not forgetting the half-can on the counter and stormed out the back door.

Within one week Tony was charging neighbors a quarter each for every mouse caught in their houses and garages. He was so good at it that sometimes he'd trap the same mouse twice.

Tony Carlito was eight years old when the family dog Goldie had puppies. The nearest anyone could figure was they were half Lab, half Golden, as in Golden Retriever. Bart, the Chocolate two doors down was the suspected father.

"Bring me that basket of dogs, boy," the father demanded.

"What are you going to do with them?" Tony asked.

"Don't go askin' me a bunch a goddamn questions boy, just get me the fuckin' dogs."

Tony froze in place afraid of what his father might do, either to the dogs or him.

"Ah, for shit sakes, you gonna make me do this shit myself? Look, if it makes you feel any better they gonna be going to a good place, better than this here," he said.

Tony brought the basket of puppies to his father as he was told.

"Alright now go back in the house and clean up where they were. There's shit and piss all over, it stinks, a man has things to do," he said.

After about ten minutes of gagging on the odor and armed with a plastic grocery bag full of feces and paper towels, Tony set out for the trash. Rounding the garage towards the alley he could hear a curious thumping noise. He couldn't put his finger on it, slightly metallic, even drum like. He could also hear splashing as he drew closer to the gate.

Inside the garage Tony's father was holding two kicking puppies down deep in a water-filled trash can.

"What you lookin at boy? Grab the damn hose, it fell out. These old cans leak. I told you they was goin' to a better place didn't I? They off to dog heaven now," he laughed.

"But dad!" Tony cried.

"Too many mouths to feed round here as it is, now get the damn hose before I gotta stop and choke someone with it," he threatened.

Tony ran. That evening he walked the alley in the hopes that one of the puppies by some miracle might have escaped or survived.

The world was white paper, and he was sketched from sadness. What he found would color-in his lines forever.

Dogs have a keen sense of smell and Goldie was no exception. When he found her she was wet, upside down in the same murder can. Even though the water trickled out, it didn't happen fast enough. He stroked her lifeless tail as he sobbed.

"You go, go be with them now."

Roughly one year later he found his father in the back yard fully possessed by the demon rigor mortis wedged between a chain link fence and a rusty metal shed. He had been missing for days but nobody was looking very hard. It had been his and his mother's best few days in years. The small area was choked by weeds, seeing through from the other side would have been an impossibility, even if the neighbor's garage wasn't there.

It had been assumed he passed out and wedged into place, terminally restricting his breathing. Crying out would have been improbable. Not that anyone would have come even if they had heard him.

Years would pass before Tony could adequately embrace the joy previously subdued by the guilt of finding satisfaction in the death of his father.

Outside of his mother physically walking him into the front doors, he didn't bother much with school. He valued hard work but loved to steal, it was a sort of addiction. After a few short stints in juvenile detention Tony ended up working as an exterminator until he was let go after an accident contributed to the untimely death of a co-worker.

He was a thin man, tall but muscular without much bulge. Black hair, a large skinny nose, and pale skin gave him an undertaker vibe mixed with a relative degree of nerd.

Construction is where his strong work ethic eventually earned him a reputation for reliability. In his twenties he accepted a full time position with the trade union where he continued to perform tasks exactly as he was told regardless of their degree of difficulty or legality. He cared for no one, everything was simply business.

● ● ●

"Call 911, call 911!" No-show yelled as he ran for the AED.

He was in full panic mode as Mr. Carl worked to revive Chris.

Once Carl called it, once he gave up, No-show lost his shit.

"What? What the hell just happened?" he yelled.

"It appears Mr. Zarnecki had some sort of medical emergency that cost him his life," Mr. Carl stated as a matter of factly.

"What? No shit! What happened? How does this just happen?" No-show screamed.

Ignoring his outburst, Mr. Carl spoke quietly into the ears of Red Shoes first and then Mrs. Smith. Under his direction they went about lifting Chris onto the stainless cart.

"I think it imperative to get Mr. Zarnecki to a qualified doctor as soon as possible for the official declaration. Emergency personnel undoubtedly will lack the clearance to be here in this place so we will move the body to a common entrance immediately," Carl said.

"Wait! You can't just roll him out on a, on a goddamned food cart!"

"Mr. Hansen, I assure you it is going to be in everyone's best interest to expedite this situation as quickly and quietly as possible," Mr. Carl said.

"Yeah? What the hell man? That big ole cart, that's pretty convenient huh? And ya'll got a couple of people here. They got clearance right? Paramedics, no, they gotta meet at the door but a clown? A maid? Your dear old mother? I'm calling bullshit man, I'm calling major fucking bullshit," No-show screamed.

"Now everybody just calm down," Daniel intervened.

"Everybody? By everybody you mean me, right? Not this, this—"

"Why Mr. Hansen what exactly are you so very clearly trying to say?" Mr. Carl asked.

"You know damn well what I'm saying, and you know damn well why too. Spy, fuckin' spy. This shit won't wash, no way. I swear to God I'll blow this thing all the way up, the lid off, everything! What did you do? It was poison wasn't it, a poison cupcake," No-show accused.

"Why, Mr. Hansen, don't be absurd. You would think I would have dear old Mrs. Smith who is like a mother to me deliver a poison cupcake to your friend?" Carl asked mockingly. He paced with his hands clenched behind his back, figuring the crime out loud like a Sunday afternoon television detective.

"Well, let's see. It was in fact the only cupcake with a candle so it would have been quite easy to make sure only Mr. Zarnecki received the poison cupcake. A cupcake we still have in our possession as a matter of fact. Let's have a look," Carl said.

In the heat of the moment Carl flipped the cupcake out of No-show's hands and onto his keyboard where it landed most unceremoniously frosting side down.

"Isn't that always the way? I don't think we can even have that cleaned," Carl said.

He picked up the cupcake and took a healthy bite, enthusiastically chewed it for the crowd, swallowed the contents, and stood like a superhero expecting to take a bullet.

"Nope, not the cupcake," he said wiping his mouth with the provided napkin.

"Okay, what about the candle? The smoke?" No-show asked.

"Why, here it is right here," Mr. Carl said as he picked it up and twirled it in front of No-show.

"Why don't you take it to have it tested, go ahead, anything for closure."

No-show snatched it from his hands.

"Don't think I won't," he said.

"Please, keep us abreast of your findings. I'm sure your information as well as an official autopsy will tell us all we need to know concerning the untimely demise of Mr. Zarnecki. Gentlemen, my sincerest condolences. Mr. Shoes, Mrs. Smith if you would please follow, oh please, allow me."

Mr. Carl held the door open as the other two rolled Chris's body out of the room on the long cart. After being out of sight he leaned back into the room for a quick post script.

"If you'd like, I'll send someone in to clean up this mess, just let me know. Oh and one more thing, as a courtesy we will have Mr. Zarnecki's personal effects removed by end of day Friday. It should be ready for re-habitation as early as Monday morning. Thanks guys." Then he was gone.

"What the fuck man? You just gonna sit there and not say anything?" No-show screamed at Daniel.

"What do you want me to say? It was an accident No-show."

"Are you kidding me man? This is the shit we used to talk about man, evil shit! They had this shit planned! Already cleaning out his place? A fuckin' clown? Who does this? And you, you don't even seem to care," No-show broke down crying.

"Of course I care. Chris was our friend. And you know? Friends don't, I mean he did a lot for us, he was our friend," Daniel stumbled on his remorse.

"Friends don't what, Daniel? Friends don't what?"

No-show rushed him and gripped both arms of his wheelchair, pinning him in place like an aggressive, hovering bumblebee.

"Don't what man?" he demanded through clinched teeth.

"Fine! Friends don't stab each other in the back! Isn't that right? Bud?" Spit flew out of Daniel's mouth as he shouted.

No-show let go with a slight push and took two steps backwards, never breaking eye contact.

Daniel softened his voice, "Maybe you should make sure to take the day off once your birthday rolls around there buddy."

"I'll bet that wasn't as thinly veiled as you had hoped, was it? Yeah, a vacation might be just what I need. Getting hard to tell which clown is running this place." No-show turned and walked out of the office.

Chapter Twelve

Long Time No See

The weather matters. A hot cup of coffee, a cozy office with warm wood floors, fluorescent lights humming. The keyboard clicks lightly from words of empathy and wonder while wind-driven cold and stricken rain smacks the outside of a drafty window. She still had to get there though, out to the car, into the building, a few hundred steps of misery. A person doesn't ever see where they are going until they have to put their next foot down somewhere. The top of a head is a universal shield. God help you if you needed gas.

One private message waited in the weeds. She wondered about its relevance. (Was it a rabbit or a fox?)

"It has been a long time, I need to see you," Anonymous.

No picture, no posts, no history. Just an account without a name, something she didn't think was possible.

"Sorry buddy, going to need a little bit more than that," she wrote back.

"You shot me, I don't blame you," Anonymous.

She hadn't shot very many people in her life. Threatened to shoot? Sure, plenty, but actually pulling the trigger? Very few. Fewer yet was any one person who may have been shot and lived, or so she would have assumed.

"If you are who I think you are, I will gladly shoot you again," she wrote.

"I was never who you thought I was, and now I'm so much more," Anonymous.

Her keyboard spoke much more loudly now, complaining after every stroke.

"Bullshit. Prove it!" she typed.

"The first time you didn't have bullets and I would have killed you if not for your burning friend," Anonymous.

"John?" She asked.

"Not as you could ever know or recognize, but me just the same," Anonymous.

"Where did I hit you?" she wrote.

"Ear," Anonymous.

"My bad. This time it will be different. I won't bother with police, not for you. And I will find you. It's what I do, remember?" she threatened.

"I will help you. You are agitated. Using one hand increases the chance of an accidental spill on a keyboard. I recommend you put the coffee cup down and use both hands to type," Anonymous.

She spun immediately in her chair and covered every detail outside her dirty alleyway window.

"Nice trick, an educated guess," she wrote.

"Close call, or is that spittle on the screen?" Anonymous.

She wiped the small dot of wet off the center of her screen with the ring finger of her left hand.

"Black and red polish, never married," Anonymous.

She covered the camera on her laptop with her thumb. Her eyes grew wide as she strained to see behind her, unconvinced as to his location.

"Of course I'm not behind you. I am here, inside the machine, inside every machine. What you see on connected glass is me looking at you any moment I choose. I can touch you, I can feel you and I need you, because he's coming. He's coming to call on you because he also needs you. He has found you because I have led him to you. I have been watching him for some time," Anonymous.

Philippine slammed the lid of her laptop closed hard enough to make her worry if she cracked the glass.

"I gotta make a…" she said to herself.

She slid her phone from her back pocket and scrolled to the call screen. After punching in the first number the screen went black. In the center of the screen, a faint pinpoint of light slowly grew. The illusion was that it was something coming closer. She watched carefully as the dot enlarged to one singular human eye, a stark raving blue eye, an eye that she had seen before.

"No fuckin' way," she said out loud.

She tried desperately to sweep it off the screen. It was in that instant that her entire office went dark. Not just someone turned the lights out dark, but more like in a box underground dark. Much to her horror, a distant point of light presented itself and began to slowly grow.

Jesus Lord I hope to hell that thing doesn't turn into some sort of damn giant eyeball.

As it grew it appeared to be a scene, a scene that would fully immerse her as an observer on a stage unnoticed by the players. She saw herself firing into the smoke as her mannequin friend melted into her childhood. She saw the John she remembered from that night run away after she shot at him.

In the next scene she was behind someone else's eyes, hiking in the wilderness, falling into cold water, fighting to stay alive. Next she came upon a house built into a waterfall, deep in an unknown forest before coming back to that spot in the water and seeing him, John, lifeless below the surface.

"Why are you showing me this?" she shouted.

"To show you, to prove to you that I have changed, that I am no longer the man John, a man who I never was. I am truth now more than ever before. I am vengeance with power known only to angels who also never were."

The world she was in returned to black.

"Look, I don't know if you drugged me or gassed me or what, but when I wake up I'm coming for you, with everything I got I will guarantee—"

The voice spoke over her, yet she had yet to realize that it made no sound.

"When you touched the screen, you touched me. Do you remember the feeling? It wasn't the first time after all, at the mall, even back when we were children on the island, we are hopelessly intertwined, you and I. Almost as if our lives were written together in a series of dime store novels."

"That's impossible. How could you know about the—? No, it couldn't have been," she said.

"You of all people know nothing is truly impossible. What you've done, what you've seen, it's the reason I need you now."

"Need me? Need me? A sadistic murdering son-of-a-bitch? What in the hell could you possibly need me for? And in what world do you think I would actually help you?" she asked.

"This world Philippine, my world. And you will because I know you, because you owe me. It was me who struck vengeance on your behalf. I was the one who killed the woman who killed your mother, the same woman who took him away."

"Took who away?" she asked.

"Come now, let's not mince. She killed your mother, she took him and eventually she killed him too. That's how he made his way back to you. She incidentally freed him. And quite the harrowing journey it was. What he is now, you will need the shock of his existence to convince them."

The black space became bright from the reflected white light of a giant skull.

"The man coming to see you, keep him alive, he is good. If he was not, he would already be mine. The men who threaten him are evil, they take what does not belong to them, *who* does not belong to them. It will all be his someday, but he must learn to answer to me, as you must also."

"That ain't never gonna happen, not today, not tomorrow, not ever. And I don't care who you are, what you are, or where you are, I'm comin' for ya, and then all this shit gonna end," she threatened.

She was back in her office, back underneath the humming lights standing in front of her desk.

"You can bet on it, John. Bet on that shit!" she yelled.

A subtle knock on the door led to temporary embarrassment after she beckoned the individual to enter.

"Excuse me, um, rather heated phone call," she explained.

"How can I help you?"

"Um high, my name is Tyler, Tyler Hansen, and after doing some research, I think you might be the only person who can help me."

● ● ●

"I guess we know everything we need to know, he isn't with us after all," Daniel said.

Mr. Tony Carlito, or Mr. Carl for short, stood at attention near the door inside of Daniel's office.

"Would you care for a drink, Mr. Carl?" Daniel asked.

"No thank you."

Daniel rolled up to the mini bar in his office and poured himself a drink, straight booze, no ice.

"How would you describe this situation? I mean, what would you do? With the programmers we have on staff…as a matter of need, as a matter of necessity, his presence is well…not necessarily necessary. Know what I mean?" Daniel asked.

"We know it was Mr. Zarnecki who contacted the FCC, and he did not work alone. And yes, we have some degree of control over the media, but Mr. Hansen's threats of exposure were not well received. These are facts," Carl countered.

"It's not something I would have ever intended to plan, I mean after all, we—"

"You should know, I called a meeting," Carl said abruptly.

"When?"

A knock on the office door answered Daniel's question.

"Mr. Hansen, how convenient as we were just talking about you. Won't you come in? And who is this?" Mr. Carl asked.

No-show stood outside the door next to a tall, thin woman wearing a long leather coat and blue jeans. Her jet black hair seemed even more so with a sharply contrasting mallen streak that made the right side of her body appear somehow stronger than her left. It was a well-lit billboard on a busy highway declaring confidence and a celebration of experience. Her boots stayed in the back of your eyes like a flash from a camera.

"Gentlemen, I'd like to introduce you to my lawyer," No-Show answered.

"Philippine, Philippine Maximine, pleasure to meet you both. You must be Daniel Navarro, Mr. Hansen has told me all about you. And you would of course be Mr. Carl," she said walking into the room.

"And I'm sure he's told you all about me as well," Mr. Carl quipped.

Her eyes looked like she wanted to smile but below her nose she was stoic. She stared at him until there was discomfort in the room. She placed a leather bag instead of a briefcase on the corner of Daniel's desk. "He didn't need to."

"What can we do for you today Miss? Mrs.?" Daniel asked.

"Philippine will be fine."

"Well, Philippine will be fine. This is a classified facility and by bringing you here, Mr. Hansen has seriously jeopardized the security."

"Mr. Hansen has jeopardized nothing. I can assure you Mr. Carl, I possess a security clearance commensurate with the highest level agents presently deployed on this planet. This is, of course, the reason Mr. Hansen did not need to tell me a thing about you. I already know all I need to know," she said.

"Of course you wouldn't mind if I were to verify your claim," Carl said.

"I'm not sure I could take your role here seriously if you didn't Mr. Carlito," she said confidently.

"Excellent, now then, I, well if you would excuse me, I shall return momentarily."

After the appropriate amount of awkwardly silent moments had passed, Philippine held her right arm high in the air, as high as she could reach. Her hand was palm down, level with the ceiling. She held it there for some time, glancing back and forth between Daniel and No-show, then back at her hand.

"I can't help but wonder what sort of point you are trying to get across right now," Daniel said.

She did not answer him, not until Mr. Carl came back into the room to join the perplexity.

"Gentlemen, this is my level, and it is many. First of all it is my level of give a crap when it comes to your feelings or excuses. It is also my level of candor as you may have already noticed. It is my level of achievement, my level of pride, and my level of confidence as a woman in a world where you have probably never seen a woman before. And that, gentlemen, is because this is also the level of shit I have seen that you would very simply not believe was either real or imagined. Finally, as Mr. Carl can now confirm that shit I was talking about has led to a security clearance which is also consequently at this level."

She slapped her hand down on the conference table. "What do you say we get down to business? Why did you kill Chris Zarnecki and threaten to do the same to my client?"

Chapter Thirteen

Huge

"Those are very serious accusations Ms. Maximine. I certainly hope you can prove them beyond reasonable doubt. In fact, I think we are going to have to ask you and your client to leave the premises immediately," Mr. Carl demanded.

Philippine laughed and sat down in one of the luxury chairs around the small conference table. She leaned it way back, any further and she would have probably fell. She slammed both boots on the table and produced what appeared to be an ordinary penny. Holding the penny between her thumb and forefinger she studied it closely, high in the air for everyone to see.

"Call it!" she said flipping the penny onto the table.

"Excuse me?" Mr. Carl asked.

"The rules say you have to call it, now it's too late. It's heads. That's really lucky because if you had called tails, and it was tails, this whole thing would have been much harder to explain. Pick it up," she said.

"I suppose next you're going to tell me what I won," Mr. Carlito said.

"Look at it closely, go ahead, I dare you," she said.

He stared at the penny but was unimpressed.

"It is as ordinary as your schtick," he said.

"Look again, only closer."

After another quick study Mr. Carl repelled and tossed the coin back onto the table. It spun in place for an extraordinarily long time.

"Cute trick, I'll admit it startled me, but I fail to see how a magic prop coin relates in any way to your grandiose accusations," he said.

"You see a penny, with Ole Abe turning his head and winking at you and you think it's a trick? I get that, you're a tough nut. Got any pictures in your wallet? What about those over there, on the shelves. Wait, I have an idea. What about a bill, pull one out I dare you," she chided.

"I have a bill. I want to see this," Daniel said rolling up to the conversation.

He reached into his wallet, pulled out a five, and slid it onto the table.

"Oh good, another Lincoln. Perfect, that's one of his favorites. Hold on to your asses."

An unnaturally blinding light shot from the penny and drowned out the room. Just as quickly it was absorbed into the five dollar bill from Daniel's wallet.

"Have a look," Philippine said.

Daniel picked up the bill and was astonished to see Abraham Lincoln smiling and winking at him. He was even mouthing words but made no sound because currency cannot speak out loud.

"Gentlemen, let me introduce you to a friend of mine. Today, we'll call him, hmmm, Lincoln. Tomorrow, we might call him your mother, your wife, or any picture you might hold dear. He could be the mannequin in the store where you try on your gaudy suits, or the talking doll Santa brought last Christmas. It took a while, I mean there were some ups and downs, but Lincoln can take over just about any human depiction he wants to be." She laughed unashamed.

"Can you imagine a Macy's Parade Spider guy chasing you through the streets of Manhattan?" she laughed again.

"Once again, nice trick, but I fail to—"

"Hold on to your hat, Carl. You see what's going to happen is our little Lincoln is going to go for a nice ride along here with our Mr. Hansen. The same Mr. Hansen who will be safely exiting this building today yet still remain a controlling member of this company. You will not see Mr. Hansen or hear from Mr. Hansen. For all you know he will have dropped off the face of the Earth, besides his formidable paycheck anyways," she explained.

"Is this what you want No-Show? Because you could have come in here and talked to us without all this, this theatre. I mean, her and her magic penny aren't really any sort of threat to us, why would you think something so childish and diluted would help you at all?" Daniel asked angrily.

Mr. Carlito, making no effort to hide the fact, spoke softly into an apparent microphone in his watch.

The bright lite shifted back into the coin. Philippine pried it up off the table with her fingernail and flipped it to No-Show.

"As a coin, of course, Lincoln is harmless. But, I mean, he could just as easily be a giant robot that most people would think was nothing more than clever advertising for the next Giant-Robot-Taking-Over-the-World sort of movie. Not you though, you would know better wouldn't you, Mr. Carl? Especially when it was standing behind your car. You might want to ask your little watch about that."

"Also, Lincoln as it turns out is one hell of a messenger. He can see, he can hear, and damned if he wouldn't be able to tell if something horrible happened to Mr. Hansen here, even if he is in his pocket, or maybe his shoe. And then, then gentlemen your problems will get a whole lot bigger than you could have ever anticipated, because then you gotta deal with him," Philippine pointed at random to every computer screen in the control room.

Philippine and No-Show put their fingers in their ears and their heads down. An ear-piercing tone took over the air, from every speaker whether they were turned on or not. All the screens appeared to crack and high-pitched screams of terror from a child replaced the tone. Finally distant laughter as the cracks faded into an illusion, into the face of Baron Samedi, the God of Death.

"My God. Show how are you even doing this!" Daniel demanded.

No-show could not hear him as he was doing as instructed, taking all course not to see or hear it, for fear that it may inhabit his soul.

A misty hand, like some sort of intelligent fog emerged out of the closest screen and took the rough shape of large fingers. It grabbed Daniel around his throat and propelled him backwards sending him crashing into the wall. He struck the back of his head and fell out of his chair, concussed and helpless on the ground. Mr. Carl was laid flat on his back on the conference table with the giant face of Samedi as large as the room itself inches from his own, laughing. So real was it for Carlito that his hair moved, and he could smell Samedi's rancid breath.

One vivid moment later the room returned to normal and Philippine slowly raised her head. She tapped Tyler on the shoulder motioning to him that it was okay for him to observe once again.

"And that, gentlemen, isn't even the one you have to worry about," she informed them.

Mr. Carl's and Daniel's phones both rang simultaneously. Feverish knocking greeted them outside the office door. Mr. Carl stepped out and after a short conversation with multiple people, back in again.

"It seems as if our experience was no fluke. The face was seen everywhere, by everyone who was plugged into our server, either now or ever," Mr. Carl explained nervously.

"That's impossible," Daniel said flabbergasted crawling back into his chair.

"How'd you do it Show? How? You're going to tell me, or I swear to God I'll, I'll..." Daniel paused.

"You'll what?" No-show asked.

Tyler stood up and straightened his shirt. "Are we done here?" he asked.

"What do you say Mr. Carl? Daniel? Do we have an agreement?" Philippine asked.

The two men stared at each other from across the room. Without any sort of explanation either logical or otherwise they nodded in agreement.

"Yes, yes we do," Daniel said defeated.

Tyler tapped the penny in his front pocket twice and made his way to the door, stopping for one final speech.

"I wanted to tell you to get out Danny, while you still can. But it's too late for that now, for any of us, too damn late."

Outside the compound, overlooking the river, Philippine and Tyler shared an unspoken *What the hell did we just see?* moment, at least, at first. Philippine removed her phone from inside her coat pocket and threw it into the river.

He stared at her for less than a long minute without her acknowledgement.

"Who's worse?" he asked.

"What? What do you mean?" Philippine heard him clearly but very simply did not want to answer.

"The Devil? Is he real?" he asked timidly.

"Honestly? I'm not sure. Is he the Devil? Maybe. I'm not sure I want to know. I almost killed him once. Tried my damndest. He's something else now, somewhere else. I don't pretend to know where that is, but I know how he can find me, find you."

"Did you owe him something? Is that why you did all this?" Tyler asked.

"I don't owe him a damn thing, except killing. He needs you Tyler, I did this for you, because he can't have you and he knows it. You have to get free from him, get off the grid while you still can."

"I. I can't just do that. It's my life. How am I supposed to get paid, buy anything? Basically live?" he asked.

Philippine smiled at him warmly and shook his hand.

"Good luck Tyler," she walked to her car stopping momentarily to admire the robot who casually walked into the lot under the cover of darkness.

"Wait, what if they come for me?" he yelled.

"They won't. Besides, he's watching you now, he's your new guardian angel. I'm sure he'll be in touch."

● ● ●

"Do we have any idea where they've gone ,Mr. Carl?" Daniel asked.

"It's been three weeks, we have some idea but as far as we can accurately surmise he has completely disappeared. He is, however, keeping his end of the bargain. He accesses his accounts remotely and doing an extremely thorough job of covering his tracks," Carl said.

"And still, we have no idea how he was able to pull that off?"

"No sir, not a clue. Not one person from the NSA, FBI, or the best and most experienced convoluted computer minds to whom we have access can tell me anything besides the impossibility of the event," Carl explained.

"And her?"

"She is by all accounts back to work as usual although decidedly disconnected. She has switched to a land-line, has no cell phone, no cell carrier, and no new computer history of any kind. She has cut herself off from the digital world. No cable or satellite TV, nothing. I would venture a guess that whatever she unleashed that day alarmed her just as much as it did us."

"Interesting. After everything we found out about her I'm surprised she'd be afraid of anything, but clearly..." Daniel thought aloud.

"If I may, Mr. Navarro, there is other pressing business. A job, high profile, unlike anything we've done before," Carl said.

"How high?"

"The highest. That is. Besides those who wish to employ our services. I guess we could call them a collective, but they've been referred to by many names."

"Can you give me a hint?" Daniel asked impatiently.

"Well, some would say he's the number one troll in all of social media, the world probably," Carl said.

"You don't mean…"

"Yes I do Mr. Navarro, and let me tell you, it would be the best hunt ever, we would use our best people, it would be huge, absolutely huge," Carl mocked.

"I want to be involved with this one myself. Full immersion," Daniel said.

"Are you sure? You could be sacrificing plausible deniability," Carl informed.

"Hell yes I'm sure. I take this clown down and I'll be a frickin' hero. A hero. Hell, I might even run for office. Let's get the ball rolling!"

Chapter Fourteen

Where in the Hell

Have You Been?

I never knew how much I wanted Esq. on my business card, but there it was. My name, Philippine Maximine P.I. had been stenciled on the glass of my office door for as long as I could remember. There were new words now, three to be exact, Attorney at Law. Everything else became implied and unnecessary. P.I., or private investigator was now a service "we", as in "I" could provide except for the billable hours get paid to an esquire at a decidedly higher rate. What I like most about that old door is that from where I was sitting, I got to read it backwards, so every time it takes a second to set in, like the back side of a bullet.

Money wasn't the only reason I did it, although admittedly it is an attractive perk. In hindsight, I became a lawyer out of self-preservation. I was in it deep, up to my eyeballs, deep enough to smell it. If I was going to do as they asked, help them find out who he was, what he was, then I needed a way to protect myself. The best defense in any government job is information. Empower yourself with information, with clout, because that's what they deal in, clout.

I was there that day when a mannequin ran through the mall under its own power. Yes, an anything but ordinary run of the mill mannequin. I was also there at the fire, with the witches. I was there when he died, at least when I thought he died. People that don't know about it intimately would never believe it. That's one of the reasons why I don't talk about it.

Over and above the supernatural experience there was a perp, somebody to chase, wounded, dangerous, a sociopath unlike any other I had ever encountered. That's when the feds got involved. I was in it, all the way, a witness as well as a suspect. I was questioned, doubted and ridiculed before I became an asset. The time I spent hanging on the rake over their coals brought something back in me, or to me, a past, a better explanation as to who I was.

I had to have blocked it all out, some sort of defense mechanism, but the memory of it seemed so new. All at once I saw new pictures of my childhood scroll by in my mind, every moment brilliantly.

I knew him, the perp but only briefly, both as a man and as a boy. It was the eyes that gave it away. I wonder how many humans a person would have to dig through in order to find two with such distinctly colored eyes. The brightness and depth of the blue was mesmerizing. I wondered if he knew who I was when we met as adults, and if he did, why did he try to kill me? When we were children, he was one of the few who bothered to help me.

The other was The Skeleton Man, a Halloween depiction come to life. The best friend of a little girl who desperately needed someone in an impossible time. A girl who lost her mother and nearly her life.

The government was looking for the skeleton, even back then. He disappeared after the event, dismissed as bayou folklore. Now, as far as they were concerned, the odds of me having contact with two inanimate objects that happened to take on lives of their own were insurmountable. Post that very important realization, I was stuck being involved for good.

Me? I thought he was gone forever. Many years had passed since I saw him burn away. John was never found, disappearing without a trace. I did what I could, but it was very much like tracking a ghost no one had ever seen. He remains near the bottom of a long forgotten wanted list. He shares the probability of being located with whoever ran over the order speaker at the drive through of the local taco stand fifteen years ago.

As far as watching him die, I was of course mistaken. Turns out he wasn't really gone, Skeleton Man, just delayed by a few years. It was a journey as unbelievable as creation. A journey that once detailed, explained to me why I remembered him in the first place.

There were rules, at least in the beginning when he was first cursed. That vague set of rules put in place by a vengeful witch were meant to confuse, torture, and teach a lesson to the man who at the time richly deserved it. Through no fault of her own, the game was changed by outside forces and a difficult spell was bastardized into an impossible creation.

He was in a man's body, trapped inside as much by his own inability to comprehend his reality as by an overbearing crazy cannibal wife who mentally and physically broke him to his core. He became increasingly unhealthy, even weak. It was mid-winter and game was scarce. The snow kept coming followed by high winds and bitter cold. Protein was tough to come by and for her, there really was no decision to be made at all. The man she knew was gone a long time ago, this thing before her was just a vessel over-flowing with simplicity in the form of a little girl's best friend she got stuck with via a bad deal with a demon. So ,of course, she killed and ate him.

He had been a plastic store mannequin, a CPR Dummy, a decorative skeleton, and even a man. This was the first time he was a picture. He could move the limbs, even the head a little, but could not make any sort of noise, nor was he free to move about the stone. The picture needed to be firmly in place.

It was the Forest Service that found him first. More specifically it was an ever increasing barrage of campers reporting moving pictographs who then reported the phenomenon to the Forest Service who found him first. A collaborative effort.

The original witch never had any intention of him landing in any human body other than his own. That feat was accomplished by a different witch, his wife, the one who would eventually murder him.

Once freed, he noticed the difference immediately. There was no flash of light, no instant awakening in a different body somewhere else. Instead, he floated freely above the ground, more aware and more intelligent than he could ever remember himself to be. By some freak accident, or grotesque marriage of spirit and nature, he had become manipulated into a traveling soul.

Like I said, there were rules, but the game changed. Therefore the rules bent, although some of the hard and fast foundations remained. Like number one, he had to exist in a depiction of a human. The bend was now it could be in any two-dimensional picture or likeness. Rule two was much more malleable. In a nutshell, he didn't have a choice, like the pictographs. After she killed him, sure he was a free soul, but he was being drawn to the first available human depiction, which of course were the pictographs, he just didn't know that it at the time. The bend of the already soft rule is that with time and practice, he could learn to move about on his own and choose his own vessel.

So there he is, kicking his legs and waving his arms in all his bear grease iron oxide ancient pigment glory on a slab of Precambrian granite overlooking an oft used waterfall trail. The popular canoe route was a harsh whisper away from the Canadian border on the tippy top of Minnesota.

People came from all over to witness the miraculous spectacle. Religious types were first to come down on twelve sides of the argument. God was real and trying to reach out, God was fake because the original artists didn't even know he existed. God wasn't the real God after all, the artist's God was, etcetera.

Next the indigenous came in hard and fast as they were the original artists. Traditionalists flocked to the scene paddling birchbark canoes, performing rituals and reconnecting with a long lost love for the land that had been stripped from them as a people generations ago.

The issue for the government, at first, was too many people. The area is only accessible by permit for the majority of the calendar year and too many were ignoring the necessity. That's when they shut it all down, the whole enchilada. Somewhere, a government guy recalling the good old days managed to string two and two together and the idea of an inanimate object coming to life jarred something loose in his memory banks.

Bought and paid for government scientists converged on the scene brimming with pre-conceived hypotheses. Once they figured out how to communicate, it told them it saw me, up there, in the woods not too long ago and it wanted to see me again.

It all happened after the fire. I saw him burn, flash into a brilliant light and die. For him it was a mere instant. He wakes up in the body of a skeleton but somehow in an earlier time, in the middle of my childhood. For him, he existed in a linear timeline, the mall, the fire, and then on to the past. For me, when I investigated the disappearances at the mall, his involvement in my childhood hadn't happened yet. The whole time I knew him before I saw him die he hadn't existed in my past so there was no way to remember him.

This was the reason why the memories came flooding back to me all at once, they were in essence, new.

Now that I know it was him, I remembered our recent encounter. I realize why he stared at me the way he did back when I saw him on that portage trail. So much so that I even told him at the time that he was making me uncomfortable. That was even before I knew he had a bag of human meat he was about to share with me.

After speaking with him once we got him off the wall he told me he wasn't sure it was me at first. He hadn't seen me in some time and between the storm and the influence of his psychotic wife, it took him too long to put it all together. It was a mistake he would regret until his death which was consequently a short time later. Of course it was me, we were for some reason, on some level, connected.

We were able to string together a partnership after that. Me, a private investigator who just passed the bar, a myriad of misogynistic middle management credit and position thieves from the federal government, and him, a transferable soul who needed purpose. As it would happen, the government would have plenty of work for us. He refused to do anything without me and eventually was able to procure a very humanoid robot to inhabit for home use, a choice which made communication so much easier.

And how did we get him off the wall that day? After weighing the options of chisels and choppers to cut and carry the stone we stumbled onto the answer. All we had to do was dangle the carrot he never even knew he wanted, a choice. The toy starfighter key fob was my good luck charm. It represented one of my favorite movie characters. Skeleton Man gladly jumped on board, and he could be heard pew pewing in my pocket all the way home. I took to calling him Buddy.

Chapter Fifteen

Trust Me

"There's no way, who does he think he's kidding?"

"This guy is a laughing stock, what a maroon."

"It's all about the money for this guy, it's nothing but a grift."

"He doesn't stand a chance, does he?"

"Wouldn't it be funny if…"

That was just a spattering of person-on-the-street interview answers regarding the Trust run for the White house. Trust, one of the richest men in America has officially thrown his hat into the ring under the guise of reviving a sleeping country. And yes, Trust was his real name.

Francis Ulysses Trust, entrepreneur, a candidate like no other. A man of the people, by the people. A self-made billionaire and a colorized picture of the American dream. To be fair, certain hues had to be added later due to the original print existing exclusively in black and white.

Like most old pictures, the edges were tattered, burned in places, and cut off in others. Creases exposed white bones and begged the question of why it was ever folded and hidden in a book in the first place. For Trust, metaphorical pictures exposed the past, the origin story of the family fortune. Making whiskey was the same as brewing money, back when prohibition ruled the land, back when the risk was worth the cost.

Old man Trust figured it out earlier than most. He understood his customer base. Judges, cops, businessmen of every ilk, and the women who dug in their heels and backed up the artificial mountain of decent society. They were dogs who never hesitated to bite because there was always another hand in line waiting to feed them. Trust fed them and fed them well.

He put forth great effort as well as an exorbitant amount of time learning the intricacies of competing moonshiner and bootlegger operations. Whenever the big dogs with badges got hungry, or needed to bark out loud, he would feed them. A delivery here, a still sight there, and never an informant to be found alive.

Eventually his ruthless business practices paid off and he was the only game in town. Once competition ran out he went as far as to set up sacrificial stills full of subpar liquor to satisfy the thirst of justice. Men on site were usually promised a payoff once they were released from prison only to be killed inside by lifers who were cheaper to buy. Trust knew how to make the best deals.

By the time the 21st amendment passed, Trust had built a fortune in political favors, real estate and good old fashioned capitol. As natural progression would dictate, on December 6th, 1933, Trust

Whiskey Distillery was born launching one of the great product and political oxymorons in the history of humankind.

The "Trust Me" campaign was more than just an obvious slogan, it was a movement. Yard signs, flags, hats, bumper stickers, it was everywhere. The bandwagon was quickly being crushed by the weight of those who were convinced they finally had a voice, a sympathetic king who heard their cries of an unfair world. Apostles lined up by the thousands, filling stadiums and celebrating his arrival on level with the second coming of Christ.

The deepest impact of the Trust Me movement came from the poison-tipped spear of social media. Trust exploited the medium like no other candidate ever had. Sycophants rejoiced in the glory that was constant communication with their savior while any sort of message became irrelevant. Regardless of his words, opponents became increasingly and often theatrically horrified and sought to have him removed from all platforms as a threat to democracy.

● ● ●

"This case is going to have to be handled differently than the way we are accustomed to operating," Carl explained to Daniel.

"Obviously, we can't just dox a candidate for president. The amount of scrutiny he faces means everything he says and does is already being paid attention to. What exactly is being requested of us?" Daniel asked.

"What you created here gives us a unique ability to strike in real time. Instead of point, counterpoint arguments, we flood the media with an answer before the question is ever asked."

"So, spy in other words," Daniel said wryly.

Mr. Carl continued on as if he never heard him.

"We have the ability to intercept a post to a number of outlets and delay its publication. Once the court of public opinion has been in session long enough the damage will already be done. If they claim their message is being purposely delayed the tech companies will have all the plausible deniability they will ever need. We can make sure those who say otherwise will appear to be crackpot conspiracy theorists no one takes seriously. We will leak information, we will learn strategy, and with the information we provide, save our country from the Trust Doctrine that would decimate what we've taken so long to build. Generations of patriots working tirelessly behind the scenes, far away from any spotlight or gold watch award dinner, all to insure the sanctity of the American way."

"The American way of what?" Daniel asked.

"Thinking, thinking, dreaming. Aren't you the perfect example of a man living the American dream? Overcame poverty, prejudice, a life-changing injury, only to become one of the richest men in the world Daniel?"

"Wait, first of all I was never poor, I may have been bullied and we all know how that worked out. But I wasn't poor. My parents worked hard to see I had whatever I needed. I can never repay them for all they have done for me. Secondly, I mean, that's what this company was built for, to stop online bullies. This, this seems wrong. This looks like we're the bullies," Daniel said.

"What this looks like is us doing what's best for everyone involved. You've heard him, heard his rhetoric, he hates people like you. You think he has any respect for you? Roll up to him at any given time, if they even let you get close. Ask him something, ask him anything. Look hard at the distain in his eyes, pay attention to the way he treats you. Then let him find out who you are, how much money you have and watch him change his tune. This guy is a professional bully and he's out of control. He needs to be stopped and we may be the only ones with the means necessary to make that happen. There's no way we can let this man become the president, no way. Trust in charge means we are extinct. This company would never be allowed to operate the way it has in the past. You don't think he'd have the government take control? You, me, everything, done. It's simple self-preservation."

"Do we have to do it? What if we say no?" Daniel asked.

Mr. Carl's face fell into clay.

"These are not people we can say no to. Take this as less of a request and more like directions. Administrations come and go, dictators, presidents, doesn't matter. These people have been there since the very beginning. These are not puppet masters and let me make this very clear to you and think about the words. They make the puppets," Carl said.

"Right, ghost stories, conspiracy theories. The Illuminati right? I'm not buying it. I've dealt with government. Intelligence is the exception rather than the rule," Daniel said.

"You are, of course, referring to Senator Domingo. Imagine what the good senator would say if he ever found out that you, Mr. Navarro, were the person who drove his son Marcus to his death to further his own business interests," Carl threatened.

"No, that never happened. That boy was ill, besides, we found the guy," Daniel denied.

"That's a lie, Mr. Navarro. You were on a personal crusade to seek justice. And not for that boy Marcus, or any other person for that matter. You've never forgiven anyone for your condition. The hate has built inside you for years. So much that you would choose death for people you once called friends. Consider that fact for a moment, Mr. Navarro. How does it feel to be the bully now? Do you think your funding was just good luck? Do you think we'd let that wack job Domingo get away with this crap if we didn't know you would be beneficial to our cause? Why do you think we chose you, Daniel?" Carl lambasted.

"Cause? Just what is your cause?" Daniel demanded.

"Self-preservation at the highest level, no exceptions. You will contribute to the best of your unique abilities to assist us with our primary goals, as well as sustain the normal function of your company, Mr. Navarro. Under the current circumstances, you would be a fool, and you are definitely not that, to believe that you are in any way in charge of this company any longer. And the public will not know," Carl explained.

"Bullshit, you can kill me then," Daniel drew the line.

Mr. Carlito froze in place midway to the door, trapped in his own thought. He jerked his head backwards as if his eyebrows both caught on hooks and string tied to the ceiling.

"Death is so final. It is really why people commit suicide. For obvious reasons, those considering such are told that it solves nothing but as we well know, they are completely wrong. Death would mean your problems were over. In good conscience we just can't let that happen, your suicide I mean. Instead, we believe adversity in one's life helps them build a stronger character. We would be glad to help you find such adversity. You say there's no way you could repay your parents? I guarantee your decision regarding this matter will have a direct impact on how they feel about your attempted installments. I trust this is clear to you now," Carl said leaving.

I always hated flies. Their persistence, the noise, they are infuriating. People made them worse. A hundred thousand generations landed where they could be killed. It was the ones who learned to bite the back of the arm that prospered, that evolved. A person can't reach around quickly enough, they take your blood, and they are gone.

Yet here I was, listening to men talk from behind the curtain, like a common fly. I am a fool taken in by fear of the unknown and shallow promises. So much power but yet I had nothing, a fake rich man upside down in debt.

These two men of supposed power spoke as if I had never existed, as if they had not seen what I had shown them. These men were fools, playthings who refuse to understand they are made of plastic. In the bush I would have used them as food for trees. Here, I will use them as food for my power and he will lord over me no more.

I was with Trust at once. His stamp in name alone on the electronic universe was massive. I followed him backwards up and through a trail of lightning to the source, only to find it was not even his hand making the words. The man hired others to do his bidding. Genuflecting souls at work sans independent thought is an existence worse than I could ever offer.

And so like I was once prone to do, I wait and listen. Keen to the intentions of both sides. I will play them as I need to, in order to get out from under him. I will use him as a human plow to sew my seeds so deep their hatred for each other will spawn worldwide discourse. Then I will harvest a more formidable force than his voodoo prayers could ever hope to enjoy.

I will be a fly no more.

Chapter Sixteen

You're Beautiful, and

You're Mine

Trust was tireless, hosting 12 rallies in as many cities in only eight days. Opponents publicly speculated a man of his advanced years would never be able to keep up such a tireless pace. The criticism was by and large tissue paper wishful thinking laid over a course foundation of praying for death by exhaustion. In slightly more than a week he has conservatively hosted a total audience in excess of 60,000 flag-waving souls.

His message resonated with a higher-than-expected percentage of the population, a number significant enough to focus the attention of the competition. Something had to be done and nothing was off the table.

Another city, another state, Trust's rallies were only limited by the size of nearby airports. His personal 757 needed a minimum of 7,000 feet to stop if everything unfolded acceptably. This Saturday late night flight was to take off into a steady north wind before veering towards the west in order to be front and center to support Wyoming ranchers. Their fight to keep their grazing lands from being swallowed by the federal government had recently gained national attention when one of their own were gunned down by representatives of said government.

The staff was exhausted after another successful appearance, looking forward to what had become a recent tradition, celebratory drinks once the plane leveled off. Including Trust and the crew of the plane, there were fifteen aboard. No one noticed that the plane didn't turn, and only one staffer managed to point out how quickly he thought they arrived at cruising altitude. It wasn't until they all had at least a few that the view through the portholes harnessed everyone's attention.

"I don't feel like we're as high as we normally are," someone said.

"Yeah stuff looks closer."

"It almost seems like we're getting lower."

The captain came over the speaker requesting everyone to take their seats, including the crew. Passengers looked out in horror as objects on the ground became ever increasingly larger with each passing second. A clear indication that they were indeed flying closer to the ground.

Trust stormed up the aisle to, and through, the cockpit door demanding answers. He came out slowly, holding a phone, casting the fake smile of disbelief.

"Ladies and gentlemen, it appears something or someone has taken control of this airplane. We have no communication, we cannot steer or change altitude. God help us all," Trust dropped the mic.

Some threw their phones, some tried to reboot, still others shook them with all their might hoping somehow they might fix themselves. They were seeing what the pilot saw, what Trust saw, what played repeatedly on flat screens on the backs of the chairs, a closeup of the face of Baron Samedi, focusing in and out, close enough to see debris in his pores.

Within minutes they were skimming the ground merely a few hundred feet off the ground. As far as air traffic control was concerned they had dropped off the scope. No active transponders were engaged, and no one was able to answer their desperate pleas on the radio.

"They're not even going to let us say goodbye," Trust said buckling himself in.

Passengers sobbed and occasionally shrieked as too close for comfort miscellaneous tower lights streaked by the tiny windows. Home, business, and street lights were getting fewer and farther between, replaced by moonlight glare from night time lakes.

• • •

"Samedi, I need to see you," I spoke it out loud as far as I could tell, not really knowing if he could hear me or not.

The way out to the world through my window washed out in bright light. The slow flash was hard to look at, enough that I turned away and noticed my shadow. I saw feet stretching into legs too far away from mine to be mine. He grew from them, like a plant, from seed to demon in an instant.

"I have to go back, back to the woods."

"A deal is a deal my friend. Besides, who would give up so much power?" Samedi asked.

"It's not forever, just for a little while. Put me back out there. This man, I have to see what he's made of, I have to know more," I said.

"What? You take his soul, no questions. What do you care? He has it coming. They all got it coming," Samedi said.

"This one has the ear of millions, a collective emotion like I've not seen. They are active. They would do nearly anything for him. I could walk them right through the gate, the ultimate haul of souls," I explained.

Samedi contemplated the offer with his own greed ultimately making the decision for him.

"Very well, but you belong to me. I will come for you when I believe it to be time, now go," he demanded.

In that moment I found myself standing lakeside in the dark, the same spot where he had originally found me. In the distance were three bright lights just above the tree tops, roaring, screaming, headed right towards me.

• • •

"We hit something I swear we hit something! We hit something again!" a crew member called out.

The impacts became more and more numerous until a person could hardly count to three before encountering another. It wasn't until one of the passengers finally saw what was happening that they had a better idea of their fate.

"Trees, we're hitting treetops," he said. As he spoke the words there became too many to count. "I think we're going down!"

The plane hit the water like a huge skipping stone. The sudden deceleration whiplashed the passengers' bodies against their restraints. Bending metal called for justice as the plane bounced back up into the air. The second touch down again violently sucked the bodies forward as a wall of water erupted forward of the fuselage.

A member of the crew still strapped to a jump seat shot forward down the aisle as if he were a daredevil fired from a carnival cannon. His net was the terrorist proof steel door to the cockpit which dented but did not forfeit structural integrity. A woman in the kitchen was also killed when unsecured stainless equipment became a projectile upon the first touchdown. As it took two hits for the jump seat to fail, its occupant had a chance to watch.

With the turbines still engaged the jet porpoised ahead into the face of a dead-end bay lined with rock outcroppings and a hundred-year-old forest. Occasional boulders started to cut into the plane as they grounded out in about eight feet of water.

They were somewhere near the Canadian border. The only hint as to their direction of travel were calls to local police stations along the route reporting a jet flying too close to the ground.

It was one of the pilots who managed to open the door closest to the cockpit. As the inflatable ramp deployed, water nearly a foot deeper than the threshold of the door flushed into the fuselage.

Those lucky enough to have not suffered major trauma during the crash found the water immediately too deep to stand even though the plane was ensconced firmly on the bottom.

It was fall in the north country. Had the crash occurred in summer there would no doubt have been campers with canoes and warm fires close by to lend assistance. But this was election season, and politics blow on cold winds. Cold winds mean cold water, and temps in the mid-forty-degree range mean death by hypothermia is a strong possibility.

Panic set in rather quickly as nobody was ready for a swim. The pilot who opened the door was busy tearing up seat cushions and tossing them out the door. The other was incapacitated from a head injury sustained during the crash.

"Oh my God, I smell fuel, I think that's fuel."

A shiny slick of jet fuel was steadily spreading across the surface of the lake.

"Everybody, get to the wing, get on the wing. Somebody is already, hey help us," another man yelled.

Trust survived with minor injuries and steadfastly refused to leave the plane even after it flooded. Once the smell of fuel became apparent and the interior toys of the rich and famous began to short out en masse, he decided discretion was without a doubt the better part of valor and jumped into the icy cold water clutching a floating seat cushion.

One by one the passengers crawled up on the wing. Trust's chief of staff May Withermen did her best to bring level heads into play.

"Okay, okay, who do we have? Who's here? Sound off, we have to get ahold of ourselves here," she yelled.

"What we have to do May, is get the hell off this wing? This wing May, is full of jet fuel, the same jet fuel all over the surface of this lake, probably, if I had to make a guess anyways. So I very strongly suggest we get the hell off this wing and away from this plane," Trust asserted.

"Cathy? Where's Cathy? She was just here, she was just crawling up with me! Cathy! Cathy," Tina, another staffer cupped both hands and called for her missing friend.

"Maybe she made it to shore!" someone said.

Shore was not close, it meant at least a half hour in the cold water clinging to cushions kicking their way forwards, slow and oppressive.

● ● ●

Drowning is among the loneliest ways to die. You can be inches from anyone in the world and if they are not watching you, if their focus is anywhere else you can slip below the surface so quickly and quietly it can be as if you were simply pulled away.

A drowning person yelling for help fills their mouth with water and drowns. A drowning person frantically waving for help sinks and drowns. Drowning is quiet, it's personal. You're allowed a last thought as you get to breathe water just one time.

I thought about helping them, just for a second, to offer the hand of God. Then they would crawl up on the wing and look up and no one would be there. Instant prayers.

It had been too long since I had been able to be personal. To be lucky enough to be there, to feel the last few surges of blood pump through a vein like it's cumming, screaming through an orgasm. The muscles tense, the grip becomes immense. It was what they were feeling and could not be anything else. Of course people at large will never believe me, and it's so simple because they just don't see enough of it to make an informed decision.

She did almost make it, I had her heel at first, the same fancy high heels that were making it so difficult for her to swim. The left one broke away during her struggle and I was forced to hold her by her ankle.

It was the noise she made that turned out to be most important. Almost a scream, but only one note, no, an eighth note, maybe less. So much terror but as her mouth filled it had no way out, nowhere to go. It is with her now until the minds decide who wants it although I already knew.

● ● ●

"Everybody in the water now or you're going to die! Now!" Trust yelled.

Twelve people entered the water including Trust, the injured, and unconscious. They clung to seat cushions designed as personal flotation devices and kicked their way towards the shoreline. They had to cover just over a quarter mile of wide-open lake. Air temp was forty-two degrees and the water relatively close to the air.

The heat wave from the blast could be felt up to more than a mile away and loud enough to cause hearing damage in those half as far.

Chapter Seventeen

Nice Trip?

See You Next Fall

The plane didn't need any help to explode, but I was there. I glowed bright white from the friction, shaking at an unfathomable speed and I ignited the world around me.

Young men need adversity to grow, to become better. He needed to fight for something, a cause, a someone, an anything to give him purpose. He was shook up, tired, a little shocky, all of which could be expected.

There was heavy gauge wire in the lake, remnants of logging that took place here well over a century ago.

"Hey, hey wait up I'm caught, hold on, hey, Jesus Christ!" the man said.

The rest of the party ignored him as they were in the process of delivering their own prayers for survival.

"Oh okay, never mind, it's fine, I've got it," he tugged at the wire more rapidly.

His blue jeans were worn through near the bottom cuff, the perfect spot to attach a wire, almost more like a long and skinny round piece of metal. He struggled against its pull-back for a long minute before he decided to remove his jeans.

Clearly the young man could think on his feet, showing adaptability and a strong will to survive. I helped him further by swaying the floating cushion from his grip, allowing him to pull against water in order to strengthen his soul. His final lifeline was the blast. I could offer him no more help beyond this point. It had to be in him.

There was a slight current here as most of the lakes in the area are connected. It was just fast enough to keep the body angled underwater as long as he stayed attached to the wire, even if he bloated.

He managed one word before his mouth filled, an outstanding showing. Something like yeyt, or yout, I'm not one hundred percent sure but I will say he did it to himself. You are so much better off using that last breath for something more constructive. In his case it would have been getting those pants off, but some people are like that.

• • •

As the shock wave smacked him in the back of the head like a flat piece of lumber, he felt vindicated. Just about as fast as a person could feel like a hero, Trust was warm and fuzzy all over, a direct result of his sudden self-realization that had they not left the wing when they did, they would in fact all be dead.

An armrest from one of the seats led the charge of blast debris traveling out in front of the shockwave by a fraction of a second.

She was single, in her late thirties, and well-known and made famous as a toxic hater of the feminist movement. The armrest, although padded made a pinging sound off the back of her head. Considering everything else happening at the moment, or more notably, what was about to happen in the next moment, nobody gave it a second thought. It fell in the water so far ahead of them that it could have been mistaken as a fish jumping in the dark. She was just gone.

Another older man closer in age to Trust had a close call with a piece of shrapnel that sheared off the entire top of his right ear and left it somewhere in the lake. They all took a crack to the back of their heads, the severity of which was related to how much of their head happened to be out of the water at the time.

Of the twelve who started, seven reached an area shallow enough that they were able to walk and crawl the last hundred or so yards to shore. Three, a few degrees off the course of the others were greeted with smelly, black bog mud to trudge through. Two were dead.

The pilot and a male staffer among the seven did their best to help the man with the head injury to shore but upon arrival had determined their efforts to be a waste of time. Among the collective distressed included contusions, cuts, sprains, and a possible broken foot.

"Okay, okay, let's get a head count," May said again.

She counted with her fingers mumbling the numbers to herself. She did this at least five times, stopping in between takes to tell herself no, that it wasn't true.

"My God…" May began to cry.

"Who?" Trust asked.

"Ten, there's ten of us left," she mumbled.

"Nine now, well, alive anyways," a man said.

"No, I didn't count him. There was another man, behind you, I counted him. A few times I counted him," May said. She stepped up on a boulder and pointed to the spot where the man had been sitting.

"No May, there was no one behind me, I'm actually on the outside" he said.

"Did he look like the man on the wing? Who even was that? And I'll tell you if there is any sure-fire way they can put me away it's going to be me publicly stating that there is a man on the wing so please somebody else tell me you saw him standing out there," Trust asked.

"Definitely sir, I was surprised to see that someone was already up there, I mean I saw him for like a second and then in all the chaos I guess I didn't notice where he went," the same man said.

The pilot used one of the two flares the survivors had to start a fire on the rocky beach. Everything else in the emergency kit was immediately self-dispersed among those who suddenly needed everything from bandages to energy bars, even though most of them had already ate. There wasn't much left besides a plastic straw from something and an emergency overdose antidote.

They decided as far as fire was concerned, the bigger the better. For heat, for signal, those who were most able made multiple trips for firewood taking them progressively further from camp.

• • •

The man with the ear. Injured to be sure but still contributing to the survival of the others. He deserved a chance to make it. The other one, the man who saw me on the wing, from the water, dead weight. A narcissistic man, a man who does just enough never does enough to justify his use of resources. They would be better off without this man.

I simply showed myself to him. Me, in all my glorious wraithdome, dark, cloaked and possibly with a loathsome smell. He ran screaming into the night, which is always dangerous.

Of course he fell but he managed quite a distance from base camp first. Not so far that they couldn't hear him scream, but they would have no idea of where to find him in the dark.

His injuries were mid-level tragic considering where he was, including a broken nose and a severe laceration on the left side of his head. He grazed off a rather sharp-edged boulder and not only did it lift a portion of his scalp, but part of his skull was also most definitely exposed to the air.

I found him on the ground gripping his wound, shaking. I took up his space with my space. I showed him the terror of my eyes. I let him hear me whisper from inside his ear to run, run for the water.

And so he ran, disillusioned, bleeding into a boulder strewn creek he fell repeatedly into the cold water, twisting his fingers in between the stones. I stayed in his ear, faster, faster.

I was with him through a beaver pond and up a steep trail on the other side. On top he needed to run, to survive. There's a special moment when a person with momentum trips. Time seems to stand still as they lay-out, seemingly suspended in midair. He was able to enjoy that moment and I gave that to him. It was a terrible place, there is a drop off, a cliff. On the bottom is where they would eventually find him.

• • •

"We have to find him? What happened to him? Where is he?" May yelled.

Dr. Gerald, or the man with the ear, stumbled out of the bush with two arms full of firewood and a pair of underwear wrapped around his head for a bandage.

"I don't know what happened, he was right by me and all of a sudden he just took off running and screaming. All I know is the direction he ran," the doctor said.

Trust, recognizing the situation he was in, jumped at the chance to own a hand written label that said *Hello, my name is Hero.*

"We do, we need to find him immediately. Now, who's with me?" Trust asked.

The doctor, the pilot, May, and Trust saddled up for the search while the rest stayed behind. A middle-aged woman and younger man event coordinators, a speech writer guy, and a grossly out of shape marketing executive were deemed not physically able to contribute.

"He went this way." The doctor led the charge.

It didn't take long before the zeal for adventure and heroism wore off and the pace shrank to a crawl.

"Everybody stay close, stay together. It's hard to see anything."

"Yeah, maybe we should wait until it's light."

"It's too late for that now, call for him."

The four of them called his name into the night as they slowly and unknowingly worked their way in the direction of the cliff.

● ● ●

"You know, if it wasn't for this darn ankle, I'd be with them, looking for him," writer guy said.

"Oh yes, yes, no doubt, as would we all if we could. You with your ankle, this woman is clearly in pain internally and the young man has a most definite splint on his leg. So we wait. It is in its simplest form all we really can do at this point," the exec said.

"I for one am starving, Anybody have anything to eat?" Broken Leg asked.

"I wish."

"I could eat."

"Okay look, we have this client, their pills, he does pills, weight loss pills. My bag, they're in my bag right over there. You take them and you're not hungry anymore. Makes you feel full. I figure it's better than starving," Leg said.

"I'm in, me too, why not, I can always stand to lose a few pounds," they said collectively.

The woman did not answer.

In the dark of the forest the four stayed close, calling for the missing man, hearing nothing but echoes off the rock and boulder strewn landscape. Their way grew steep, forcing them to climb in a line in which their place was determined by their physical ability, or lack thereof. On point was the pilot, then May, the doctor, and finally Trust.

"Thank God I think this is the top. I think I can see sky," the pilot said.

The light through the forest in front of them was the sky, most highly visible from the edge of the cliff.

"Hey wait, is that? No, stop!" May screamed.

A few long bounds away from her was a shadow of a man, exactly what they were looking for, too far into the process to stop jumping to his death in front of them. May pushed past the pilot and stretched out to grab the falling man. The pilot in turn stretched out to catch her.

May went over the side and pulled the pilot along for the ride. He was able to get ahold of a few fledgling pine trees to save himself, but he was dangling. May screamed all the way to the bottom.

The doctor grabbed the pilot's arm and assumed the tug of war anchor position.

"Help me, help me!" the doctor begged.

Trust, out of breath, and gasping for air put both hands on the doctor's shoulders and tried to drag him backwards.

"No, no, not me you damn fool, help me pull his arms, no, no, you're, no!" the doctor screamed.

Pulling on the doctor's shoulders, Trust caused the doctor to lose his grip on the arms of the pilot and, in the end, gravity prevailed.

"You idiot! You killed that man! Don't you see what you did? You, you did this. We could have saved him!" the doctor berated him.

Trust stood a few feet away hunched over with his hands on his thighs, taking deep breaths, still unrecovered from the climb.

"No, I did no such thing. Where? Show me?" Trust asked.

"Why right here, right here. Are you kidding me?"

The doctor grabbed Trust by the arm harshly and stepped towards the edge pointing profusely over the side.

"Down there! Down there where you killed him!" the doctor said.

"Where? Down there?" Trust asked as he pushed him.

Like May, the doctor screamed all the way down, until he didn't.

Chapter Eighteen

The Voice

"You were a good doctor Dr. Gerald, you really were, the best and I'm very sorry that I had to do that to you but let's face it. You'd have talked. I know it, you know it. So, I'm sorry, but this is the way it has to be," Trust explained to the night air.

The light of a distant morning sun glowed from the east. Travel was easier now as Trust who had plenty of time to practice his lines, made his way back to camp.

Every person besides the oldest woman was unresponsive and not breathing. The injured woman crawling with what was left of the first aid kit was only able to loudly and forcibly whisper, "help me."

She poured the contents on the ground in front of her, two nasal doses of Naloxone, a drug that if administered in time might save their lives.

"Me? You want me? What happened here? What happened to them?" Trust demanded.

She gasped, "OD, over D—" before collapsing.

"Them? They overdosed? On what?" He checked them all quickly.

"You know what I think you might be right. I'm not even sure they're breathing. I have to tell you honestly I've never had to do anything like this before. I've always had people and I had the best people. I would never have to deal with this," Trust monologued.

After fumbling with the packaging far too long, Trust finally attempted to administer a dose.

"I guess you just put this in here and push this."

He administered most of the first dose to the youngest man through his nostril and then tried to very quickly get some into the executive as well from the same inhaler. For the next dose he did the same except most of it went to the writer with the balance once again going to the exec. Nearly immediately the three began pulling in air, rolling to their sides as they choked, and puked their ways to partial consciousness.

Trust sat hard and fast, back up against a boulder, exhausted.

"Well, looks like you're all coming around. This is as good of a time as any to tell you there's been a horrible accident, an absolutely horrible accident. Let me tell you something. This accident was so horrible that all, or alright, most other accidents pale in comparison."

Trust went on to tell them about the sudden cliff, how the pilot turned out to be the weakest link in the human chain and if not for his good fortune of owning a very expensive and the best belt ever made catching on an exposed tree root, he too would have fallen to his death.

"One of the hardest take-aways folks was if they just heeded my advice and not advanced so quickly, or even let me be the anchor, you know, clearly as the strongest man I would not have let go. I just can't abide people who let go. This could have all been avoided, our dear, dear friends," Trust explained.

What the pilots reportedly saw from the float plane that morning was a beaten down and filthy Francis Ulysses Trust heroically loading the fire with whatever he could find in order to signal the plane for help with the others laid out in a row. Pictures of the event were splattered across every smart screen in the world as details of Trust's heroic tale of survival and selfless sacrifice began to leak.

EXT. LOCAL HOSPITAL - AFTERNOON
Trust rises to the podium. More people stood outside than lived in the town, probably the entire county.

                    TRUST
            They tried to kill me!

Pause for Dramatic Effect (PDE).

                    TRUST
            But they failed!

PDE

                    TRUST
            And do you know why they failed?

PDE, mixed with shouted ridiculous answers.

                    TRUST

Because I am more than a man. I am a movement. WE are a movement. And you can't kill a movement so easily.

PDE and chants of USA.

> TRUST
> But they did manage to kill some good people, some great people as a matter of fact. The best. And I would like you to join me now in a moment of silence to honor and remember their heroism.

Quiet PDE.

> TRUST
> Let us also say a prayer or prayers, many prayers is good, for those who survived, everything from the initial crash to accidental poisoning, even internal injuries, all injuries, they were all injured, very badly, in some cases, very badly. Let's pray for them as well.

PDE long enough for an extremely short silent prayer.

> TRUST
> Today is the first day of the rest of this campaign and I tell you, no, I promise you, we will survive! We will go on! We will win! And not because of votes

alone,   but   because   we   are
survivors! We are the explorers
of the new world! We are winners!
Together! Thank you!

CROWD - Raucous applause, chanting,
potential clothing removal and launch.

Conspiracy theories were many and were highly encouraged by the candidate and the campaign in general. It was all out *us versus them* for the Trust camp. A common business man against big government lifetime politicians. A David self-made giant versus the even larger Goliath who was buried too deep in shit or denial to notice he was getting viciously pummeled in the court of public opinion.

The hordes who said he could not win fell silent. The polls were generous but even they couldn't cover up the surge. Every city, every town, postal code, and tourist trap had at least one person that believed whole-heartedly that Trust would die for them, and in some cases, many, many more.

Trust rode the wave of the plane crash to double digit leads in most of the major cities across the country. It was all but a done deal. All except for one, pesky rumor. A rumor that the opposition, in light of having absolutely zero in the cannon decided to run with, just as fast and far as they could.

The idea was floated that maybe, just maybe, Trust crashed his own plane, and that's why he was one of the only people to survive. Maybe the ones who did survive were accidents? Maybe it was his way of getting rid of people who knew too much. And of course miraculously he was fine, no injuries!

Others pointed out that it would have required an expert pilot to fly a commercial jet at those altitudes, dodging towers, knowing exactly what to turn on and off in order not to be tracked.

Some questioned the validity that the jet was taken over by an unseen force in the first place. Most noting that sort of computing technology does not even exist, and if it did, considering the thousands of flights across the globe daily, could potentially be some of the most dangerous to ever exist. Without a way to stop it, global and military air travel could be thrust back to the romantically unhealthy days pre brothers Orville and Wilbur.

The obvious answer and most definitely the best way to never get to the bottom of virtually anything, was to have a full blown government investigation for as one Senator phrased it, "In the interest of an honest and fair election". Flecklessly swinging a soaked broad brush of investigative authority would give the special prosecutor the power to sequester what Trust ate for breakfast, how and how much he paid, who sold it to him, how it tasted as well as a steaming hot sample stuck in a luxury hotel toilet that wasn't allowed to flush.

The government aligned with the opposition would look at everything from inspection logs to fuel sources and focus highly on the NTSB report determining the probable cause for the crash. Witness interviews, crime scene investigations and experts in every field from wilderness hiking and adventure racing to aeronautical engineers would be gathered to help reach a consensus. The world's pre-eminent psychiatrists would dissect the behavior of each survivor post touchdown and determine, based on available reports and testimonies their probable mental states.

No price tag was deemed too high. People were being repeatedly told their democracy was at stake, especially if those who were saying it didn't win.

• • •

Mr. Carl combed the hallways a bit slower than normal that morning with noticeably less nazi enthusiasm in his gait. He walked into Daniel's office without knocking.

"Please, come in," Daniel said sarcastically.

"You requested my presence?"

"Damn right I did. Did we do this? Is this something you and your team did?" Daniel asked.

"No, we found out just like everyone else did. However, um, how shall I put this?" Mr. Carl searched the ether in the room for an answer.

"Just put it," Daniel said.

"They think we did. They know it wasn't them because they very simply don't have the technology to pull it off," Carl said.

"And we do? I am certainly not aware of any program we have even close to what would have had to happen to fly that plane remotely. Because that's what they're saying right? Someone took over control of the plane? Why do they think it was us?" Daniel became agitated.

"As far as they are concerned what we do isn't much different. We are capable of things that they are not. Why build what they can take? If there is even an inkling that we possess such technology they would seize control immediately, most likely one half hour ago," Carl explained.

"A half hour? That's suspiciously specific," Daniel noticed.

"I have just been informed. As it is they have requested full access to our system and I suggest we comply, while smiling," Carl said.

"No, no effing way. I don't like it. It's bullshit. Those programs are proprietary! They're mine! Well, mine and T's but…" Daniel froze mid-meltdown.

"Wait, they're right, sort of. What we do isn't much different after all. I mean, at the heart of it, we are controlling someone else's system. If we took it one step farther, control a system that controls a system…it's a very conceivable concept in a fly by wire system of any kind," Daniel proselytized.

"So now you think it was us?" Carl asked wryly.

"No, well, maybe yes and maybe no. If it started with us, who else could pull it off? Who else not here anymore, who has access to the programs, who makes the fucking programs? Ring any bells?" Daniel chided.

"Mr. Hansen, I presume?" Carl asked knowingly.

"Damn right Mr. Hansen you presume," Daniel broke into a laugh. "He was the damned, the damned…flight simulator ace champion," he laughed too hard to speak.

• • •

I was in the plane, in the wires, in every circuit, every twitch of electricity, I flowed through it, controlled it. I became a conduit. My new friend pushed the buttons, sent the commands while I was as blood carrying oxygen to the brain of the airplane.

"Please, tell me this is the end of this. I did this favor for you and now it's over, right?" Tyler wrote.

The letters on Tyler's screen disappeared as quickly as his fingers moved off the keys.

I could see Tyler's message as the letters he typed assembled themselves in my thoughts as sounds only I could hear. When I speak to him I do it through these letters and they appear for him. On this day, I wanted to hear my voice.

It was electric and old fashioned. It sounded grizzled and slow. A mountain man nearly froze to death, delivering his last words to a mule. I spoke slowly as it was difficult for me to process how and what I was doing as I spoke through the speakers of his machine.

"You did it to save the people on the list."

Tyler screamed obscenities, comfortable in the anonymity of an unused keyboard. He did not understand that my eyes and ears were his machine and I did not want him to.

Once he calmed down he typed a response.

"You gave me your word that they would be safe!"

"And they will be, for now," I replied.

"For now?" he asked.

"Their safety depends on you, not me."

I no longer felt as if I needed to speak with him, so I severed the connection, although I did entertain his last message.

"P.S. Can you please not speak in that voice anymore? Not sure I can sleep. Might affect my work."

Chapter Nineteen

How Did You Get In Here?

The new fences around the facility were thick-wired cyclone waffle cones topped with a generous scoop of morally abusive concertina. Jersey Barriers, concrete dividers commonly used in road construction, braced-up the backsides. Banks of high intensity generator-driven lights kept the exterior in daylight indefinitely.

The miscellaneous vehicles that used to dot the cracked-up blacktop parking area were replaced with an army base motor pool lined two stories high on all sides with shipping containers as if whoever gave the orders was preparing for a zombie apocalypse. High definition cameras bloomed like flowers on nearly every pole.

Inside Daniel Navarro's former dream facility, operations turned gestapo nearly overnight. Heavily armed guards were stationed just inside the main entrance with admittance reserved only for those with classified clearance.

The staff was largely replaced with hand-picked government employees as well as specialists from various military and civilian complexes. Daniel was among the few listed as one who may possess "inimitable contributory skills" and was spared from being exiled from his home.

The rest of the domiciles in the facility were carved up and used as barracks for the infusion of military personnel. The former residents were hastily relocated and saddled with the sort of secrecy that if broken results in charges of high treason or an unfortunate industrial accident.

For Daniel, his dream had become a prison. A cracked figurehead on a recklessly piloted ship. The first and last face you see before you get rammed.

Mr. Carl no longer bothered to knock when entering Daniel's office. "I should tell you that I have been granted full autonomy over the day-to-day operations of this facility. I am fully aware of your contributions, and I can assure you that if you so choose, your compensation for the company will be more than generous by government standards. You would have to correspond with Mr. Hansen, assuming you can locate him."

"In the meantime, your continued assistance would be invaluable. Feel free to stay as long as you may desire as you are cleared for the system at an executive level," Carl explained.

Daniel was neither surprised nor impressed and called upon all the hubris he could muster in order to contain his rage.

"The writing was on the wall. In hindsight, it was inevitable from the beginning. T was right. Who's this?" Daniel asked.

Another man entered the office but said nothing. A pale, white man, thirty five or forty years old, salt and pepper gray hair, thick and combed straight back. Average height and muscular, he was wearing all black sweater, pants, and boots. He said nothing but seemed curious as to his surroundings.

"He is Eric Jon. He's what I will call our newest specialist. As you well know, from time to time it is necessary to get some boots on the ground, some agents in the field. Jon will fit into a supervisory position, eyes on the target so to speak. Above all else we have to make sure that these things are done smoothly, without complications," Carl said.

"What things?" Daniel asked.

"Like I said, boots on the ground operations. A man at your level doesn't need to bother himself with such details," Carl said.

"What about your level? Aren't you the boss now? You're dealing with it right?" Daniel asked sarcastically.

"Absolutely not. That's what we have Mr. Jon for. So, if there's nothing else…" Mr. Carl heavily hinted his exit.

Daniel gave his best impersonation of a man who didn't believe a word of what he was just told and made sure to write it all over his own face, in pen.

"Of course you realize that makes absolutely zero sense, but there is one important thing I need to discuss with you, in private please," Daniel said glaring at Mr. Jon.

Mr. Carl gave an approving nod and Eric Jon responded with a quick and quiet departure without ever uttering a word throughout the meeting.

"Do you ever wonder how he did it? You were there, you saw it. Seems like we don't want to admit that something happened here. What the hell came out of those screens? How did he do it?" Daniel asked.

"It was obviously the woman. A trick, an illusion. False witchcraft. It was impossible, all of it. And much like your ex-friend, she's dropped off the grid. Electronically anyways," Carl said.

"Pretty believable if you ask me. And if they did it once, they can do it again," Daniel explained.

"We've already run diagnostics and found that the system operated perfectly. It was a trick. What would you have me do?" Carl said annoyed.

"Look, I know you want to move me out of here, I'm no idiot, but this is my place, my company, I built it. You guys may have paid for it, but the ideas are mine. It doesn't exist without me and if you think I'm going to willingly roll my ass out the front door you've got another thing coming. I'm not going anywhere. He hacked into my, well, our system and did some things I can't believe and damn it to hell I want to find out how he did it," Daniel said passionately.

"Fine. But remember, you report to me and me alone. I hope we are perfectly clear on that," Carl said.

"Of course. Obviously my door is always open." Daniel's sarcasm wreaked.

"Oh, and one more thing. As far as the public is concerned you are one hundred percent the face of this company. Should the need arise for media appearances and the like, you will be expected to follow specific instructions regarding protocol and our official position. It's really the best of both worlds for you. All the glory without the burden of excessive responsibility. In a way, I envy you," Carl said before quickly leaving the room.

• • •

A step inside Mr. Carlito's windowless lair was equivalent to visiting a mall security office. Facility cameras constantly refreshed views of mostly unsuspecting workers, including Daniel Navarro.

"I'm not sure he's a hundred percent on board with all this," Carl said to Mr. Jon.

"Why would he be? The guy just lost everything," Jon said.

"Not yet. There is a significant number of people in this country that see him as some sort of Robin Hood. The man who single handedly brought civility back to the internet. What those people don't realize is the level of sophistication we are constantly battling will eventually render us moot, useless. People are starting to laugh in the face of being doxed, exposed. They don't care and more and more are learning ways around our system. We shut them down and they're back within a matter of hours, minutes even."

"That's where you come in. Tell me Mr. Jon have you ever heard of the word buzz? I mean as in internet buzz. Small talk, posts, rumors, innuendos, that sort of thing. I have an initial list of seventeen people that we never want to see touch a keyboard again, ever. I believe that if we neutralize these individuals that we may indeed create that buzz."

"Healthy fear is the end goal. If they don't fear us, they will not respect us. What we have found is there is only so much that can be done electronically. You and your team will handle the physical nature of the operation. Bring back everything and anything that can be used to access the internet. And as far as the seventeen are concerned, they are to be eventually found. The higher the profile of the individual the longer that discovery is to take. The more rumors that may spawn as to their whereabouts, the better. We'll handle that end of it in house. How soon can you and your team be ready?" Carl asked.

Both men stared at the monitors, specifically at Daniel Navarro. Mr. Eric Jon seemed to be in no hurry to answer.

"Whenever you say go," he said.

"Excellent. Go," Carl answered quickly.

• • •

For weeks after the meeting Daniel combed the system looking for answers. He poured over years of painstaking code, unintentionally reviving the altruism of two young men who once shared a dream. One of those young men he wasn't having any luck finding and the people who could, would probably kill him if they did. Carl and associates eventually became bored and discontinued their surveillance, chalking up Daniel's work to a wild goose chase that only he could understand anyways.

It just doesn't make sense. How in the hell did he do it?

With some effort, Daniel physically exposed every processor to which he was currently engaged and disconnected the fans. Next he set them on task to compute an insurmountable amount of data.

Here goes nothing.

Quality construction of the electronic components slowed down the desired outcome but eventually warnings ensued. He did what he could from his side to bypass the safety measures and push the processors past the limits of their designs. The heat eventually became too much, and they started to smoke.

Daniel was full of rage and anger, his company destroyed and currently under the thumb of a tyrant, his nearly lifelong friendship in ashes, and a stack of regrets too high to climb. The smoke pulled at him, a sick game of "got your nose" perpetrated by a sociopathic wraith trapped in cyberspace. Finally a series of keystrokes, a pattern to which Daniel had given much thought and once discovered, unveiled itself as the obvious solution.

This has to be it.

After hitting enter the room lights dimmed.

Interesting.

As Daniel was waiting for something to happen on the screen in front of him he tried to find the source of a new humming sound that had simultaneously taken over the air in the room, but he was thwarted as he had carefully made sure to have nothing else running. To him it sounded like a distant machine, but with a resonance that he could feel throughout his body.

Daniel's monitor showed only blackness, like it was surveilling an empty room. Something passed by quickly from right to left, a person who very suddenly returned and much closer to the device on their side. The face on his screen faded between two, one a man and the other hidden by the shadow of a black hood. When Daniel managed to see the eyes, he recognized confusion and surprise. It surely didn't expect a party.

"You! You can see me!" the wraith spoke.

The voice was concerning to Daniel. It gave him a hollow feeling as if consorting with Satan. By this avenue he also knew at that point that he had officially made contact with whatever it was that Tyler and his lawyer used in the office that day.

Who are you? Daniel typed.

"You are one scary sounding son of a bitch," Daniel said aloud under his breath.

"Forgive me, I have only just begun to use my voice," it answered.

Daniel rolled back from the keyboard in shock, immediately understanding that it had heard him even though there was no microphone currently in use on his system. The entity looked to the side, towards the processor, which was smoking heavily, and crackling like breakfast cereal freshly bathed in milk.

"Our time is up," it said.

Daniel's computer hissed one more time and the screen went blue showing only the ghostly outline of the last thing that matched that particular color, eyes.

Chapter Twenty

The Blind

Maybe it's time to just once and for all round up all these leftist liberal commies and take our country back. Patriots unite!

The social media post heard round the world proudly posted by presidential candidate Francis Ulysses Trust.

The backlash was immediate. News agencies coordinated a global rebuttal spanning miles and languages as if the earth itself was in peril. Their shared message was eerily unified as if the script had already been written. "We are under attack from 'The Trusted'", a monicker proudly received by the many followers of Trust.

The first casualty was the social media platform itself. Guilt by association. People questioned and sneered at the buffet of chosen information on their plate as it was brought to their table. They cried for banishment, they cried for censorship. Governments and businesses around the world banned its use on their soil and time, calling it fascist, reminiscent of the work of Joseph Goebbels.

Push begat pushback and two sides, two ideologies became as militant religions fighting over the will of God. They worshipped in the churches of everyday life, scorning those who would dare eat different foods or wear different clothes. Likewise those who chose tradition were lambasted as supporters of the past, which was in their eyes inherently to blame for the great offense de jour.

Every film, every song, every food, every drink, everything was screwed into a soft wood ideology. Nothing was attached, nothing was made, not even a chair. Words and attacks were just jagged piles of boards lying about with the sharp ends of the screws exposed hoping to draw blood from anyone. Any kill was a good kill, even if it was one of their own.

If a person did not agree with something, be it nearly anything, that person was wrong. If they possessed any fact, it was a lie, and more disturbingly, vice versa. Each choir had been sufficiently preached up and minds to be changed were devalued. A person who stood on the middle ground would likely choose a side based solely on who might be their first contact. In most cases they ran in the opposite direction defeating the purposes of recruitment.

"No sir Mr. Trust. No way, no how. I wrote it, moved it to editing, then back to me before I posted it sir. I have clear email evidence, time and date stamped showing the originally planned post," the man said nervously following Trust who was wearing the floors thin in his office.

"Well, that's not what hit the wire Mr. McGinnis," Trust stated while matter-of-factly gazing out his high-rise window.

"Sir, verbatim—'Maybe it's time to just once and for all extend the olive branch, to work tirelessly to unite our country. Patriots unite!'—Patriots unite Mr. Trust, as you requested, the olive branch, again as you requested."

"Mr. Trust, there is only one plausible explanation. I had to have been hacked. Somehow, someone was able to intercept that message, change it, and post it under our account. I didn't think anything of it at the time, but the physical posting of it took some time, much longer than usual," McGinnis stared at the ground and slowly paced behind Trust.

"I mean, I chalked it up to a slow connection, it happens all the time, but not here, and I didn't think anything of it. That's when it had to have happened," he said.

"When it comes time to put your hand on the bible and swear to tell the truth, let's hope you don't forget any of those details. In the meantime, I need you to stay out of the media until we figure out how to handle this," Trust advised.

"But Mr. Trust, what about if I just tell the truth?" McGinnis asked.

"Nope, no good. They'd never believe us, trust me, we need proof," Trust paused. "Really though, you might be right. Maybe we will tell them and that we'll get proof. You know, find the killer like what's-his-name."

Trust smiled. "Oh and we will, rest assured. So you're with me, if you had plans now would be the time to adjust your schedule. Miriam will see you have everything you need."

"Miriam? Wait what, I'm not sure what you mean," McGinnis said confused.

"Yes Miriam, she's much more than a secretary or even a personal assistant. She's great, the best. You'll have the best and quietest room, well, not the best, one of the best though," Trust explained.

"What? I'm staying here? Mr. Trust, I have a wife and a young child, I…" McGinnis stammered.

Trust finally turned from the window and made his point in conjuncture with his right index finger pounding on the desk.

"I need you right now and you need me. Miriam, call Keith and have him either send someone, or better yet, go himself over to pick up Mr. McGinnis's wife and child. Set them up in a suite here in the hotel, please."

"Yes, Mr. Trust," she said.

"Out there, they can get to you. In here, we have some of the best security in the world. The best. Stay here, we'll do a press conference from downstairs," Trust said.

"Mr. McGinnis, would you follow me please?" Miriam politely asked.

Trust turned back to his window as Mr. Kelly McGinnis, Communication Director and Press Secretary for the Trust campaign followed Miriam hurriedly jaw agape through the gilded office door.

• • •

In Congress, the hand forged springs of the bandwagon were being tested to their limits.

"A house of peace through strength is built on a foundation of fear rather than respect. It is home to lies and half-truths, mistrust and anger. The architecture is distinctly Roman, it's the white columns that give it away. Did we forget these timeless words of our previous president? We need common sense gun control now!" the congressman bemoaned.

His name and district were inconsequential. He wasn't even one of the handpicked elite. More like a hopeful that thought maybe if he called a press conference and echoed some party sentiments he just might get an audience with the queen.

Guns were all the rage, good guns, bad guns, millions had one, or two or three. The good guys, the bad guys, however they identified had them in common. For the left they were a necessary evil, an invited dark figure of death looming in the corner that helped the elite feel comfortable and protected.

For the right, guns were alter pieces, lauded golden calves, black keys to salvation cut by high capacity magazines.

Spatz Clarke had a gun, many in fact. One in particular was his favorite. A big game rifle, bolt action, 30-06 Springfield. One of the most common and practical hunting rifles ever made. It held a total of five shells including the one in the chamber. A shooter needed to cycle the bolt backwards to eject the spent shell before sliding it forwards again to plant the next one so that it would be ready to fire. With the least amount of moving parts, what bolt action rifles lack in projectile capacity, they more than compensate for with accuracy and dependability.

Spatz was young, deep in his late teens when he saw an actual president in person. He was fishing from a quarter mile long concrete pier jutting into Lake Michigan in the pre-dawn early morning hours when the secret service shut down his venue. Soon the lake was littered with Coast Guard vessels clearing out any sport boat in the vicinity.

At the base of the pier was a large public park where the event was to take place. Nearly every rooftop in the small town on the hill held a trooper with a rifle. Men in generic suits with ear microphones were everywhere.

Spatz grabbed a seat up front, anxious to witness the spectacle. He was an avid outdoorsman filthy and tired with a white paper bag full of donuts. The secret service did not approve, and he was moved multiple times until he was no longer eligible for a chair. Years later the context was inconsequential, it was the experience that mattered.

Eventually, someone, one of them, is coming. And they ain't never gonna know what hit 'em.

He chose a port with historical meaning. He wanted a speech platform that was old but ornate, like a classic gazebo or Victorian bandshell. A smaller community away from a big city so it would be easier for them to secure. Most importantly it had to have a good view of the lake.

Lake Michigan holds some of the meanest water on the planet. Wave heights of an ocean storm twice as close together coming from random directions. A giant bathtub full of really cold water.

Winter storms have changed and shaped the shorelines of the lake for thousands of years. As far as cities were concerned, that is generally not a good thing. In order to protect the valuable real estate—old streets, sidewalks, porches, walls—anything made of concrete was utilized. Stacked to compliment and protect the shorter, older concrete break walls they slowly built longer and taller harbors.

Huge local deep-tunnel projects provided a nearly endless supply of car-sized limestone blocks of various dimensions that were perfect for topping the numerous walls of old jagged fill. They were able to stay white most of the year thanks to gob after gob of avian contemporary shit renderings. The cormorants and gulls made for a thought-provoking combination of styles and talents.

All a guy would have to do…

Spatz started with a wheelbarrow, covering a storage unit floor with two feet of ordinary dirt. He shaped the area about the size of a small car into random valleys of a moonscape. On top he laid out a large sheet of cardboard, making it continually damp so it would contour to the dirt below.

Piece after piece he painstakingly formed the structure into the likeness of a squared-off limestone boulder. Numbered pieces of cardboard duct taped together and mapped. Inside the structure was built to have a large section of flat floor suspended over a jagged bottom to be filled with stone.

The structure had to be waterproof, and fiberglass was the obvious choice. Spatz mimicked each panel individually, seamed them together with plaster, and painted it to match the surrounding sea wall. He built in a small door removable from the inside. Angled downwards the door was invisible from above. Once removed a screen mesh the same color as the exterior covered the hole. Smaller vent holes on the other side were similarly installed.

The entrance was inspired by a beaver lodge, through the bottom, under water. His mission would require a scuba entry and with proper provisions, he would be able to hold out inside the blind for days.

The last and largest hurdle was the physical installation of the blind. Upon completion it was bound to be quite heavy, way too much for one man to handle. Besides a crane and barge, he needed to get it out of storage and to the lake without anyone seeing it and asking any questions. As availability was an impossible commodity the only way to achieve this goal was to use someone else's equipment. For this he needed research, and time.

The Army Corps of Engineers contracts break-wall construction years in advance. Winning bidders become public knowledge. Spatz applied to the company that won the bid for his desired location as a deck hand and over time eventually worked his way onto a barge. The trade required transience, and jobs may take months to complete depending on the weather. Pay and benefits were surprisingly good and for a single man with a liveaboard boat and secure storage the match was ideal.

A thunderstorm provided perfect cover. Ineffective cameras due to power loss could not document the oddly shaped tarped object winched onto the trailer. The gull spattered antique cameras at the marina were next to useless even if they had been pointed at the lift.

After the storm a light rain persisted with a west wind that kept the waves nearshore to a minimum. Security on the barge was two men, one in a shed and one walking the deck. Spatz swam out from his slipped boat in the marina.

Earlier in the day Spatz rigged a piece of cable, stressed like a trigger from an unnatural bend. Once tripped from the water it would provide just enough force to take a man's foot from under him, preferably both. The security guard strolled the deck like a game trail, predictable, systematically. For a fraction of a second, his feet were higher than his face and he hadn't even hit the deck yet. He was for all practical purposes blacked out when he landed but Spatz added a quick hard thump for good measure.

The guard in the shed would be easier, it didn't even matter if he heard anyone coming. Spatz removed one tank from his back and slid a flat tipped hose under the door. A moment after release, he could hear the guard coughing profusely, staggering and falling as Spatz breathed the clean oxygen from his other tank.

In these few moments Spatz was able to successfully unload his faux boulder in such a way as that portion of the wall looked most obviously completed. The area Spatz chose was break wall only, inaccessible by foot or watercraft as there was no way to safely dock. The structure lived on the inside of the wall partially underwater, away from the direct fury of the lake.

The guard who fell eventually came to and found his coworker hunched over and deceased in a shed filled with foul smelling gas later determined to be the hydrogen sulfide. It was thought that the barge had somehow disturbed a pocket under the lake floor and flooded the compartment with gas. It may have even been responsible for the first guard falling as he became disorientated, unaware of the concentrations he was inhaling.

Spatz waited and watched the newswire patiently for more than two years. Then it happened, the anniversary of the sinking of a late 1800's sailing vessel that took a number of men from the town down with it. Their bodies were never recovered.

● ● ●

"Mr. Trust this is small town America, your base. If anyone is going to believe you, it's these people," McGinnis explained.

"I hope you're right Kelly. We screw this up and it could sink us," Trust smiled, his level of give a shit nearing absolute zero.

Chapter Twenty-one

And So They Prayed

Center, why wouldn't it be?

The tiny hole in the middle of the target was missing, a victim of multiple hits. Spatz liked to record five bulls per day, preferably first thing in the morning like some people have to have their coffee. The nine to five, however, often does not work in conjunction with the sun.

The Lombardi Trophy, the Stanley Cup, FIFA World Cup, The Heisman, symbols of ultimate success, the end game, the reason to set the goal. Earned by gifted people who strive for excellence. Not fit for consumption by the average human. Nobody knows who the best delivery driver is or was, and there will never be a national award for it.

Skills vary among the great unwashed. Some draw, some write, some are good with animals. Spatz hits centers, bullseyes, and it didn't matter how. Darts, jarts, bow and arrow, axes, even an atlatl. Never considering his skill unique, he never vied for a trophy of any kind, local, state or national. On multiple occasions he could not comprehend why others could be so bad, off the mark, like something was wrong with them. It was always an easy game. Accolades meant nothing and he became terminally bored with people inquiring as to the how and how many. He decided long ago he would do 'it' just to see if he could, regardless of what the 'it' was.

Spatz didn't hate anyone. To him people were non-player characters, NPC's, unused targets without sentience. A sick video game mentality that he carried over into real life. It was nothing personal. It simply didn't matter who signed up to speak in the park that day, just as long as they were high profile. At least that would make it a challenge. As far as Spatz was concerned, they all had it coming for something they did, or they wouldn't be there in the first place.

The mayor opened the festivities, the choir cheered. So many banners, hats, flags and signs, the crowd looked far more ready for a Sunday afternoon football game than a political speech. Football was big medicine in this part of the country, but it would have to wait one more day. Spatz was already on day two, having slipped into the water in the wee hours post-midnight Friday just after flipping a quarter off the stern, a habit he picked up as a good luck omen while trolling for salmon out on the main lake.

Inside the blind he stocked dry boxes with clothes, food, water and such, while his bodily waste was returned to the lake through the swim-in hatch in the floor. He tried not to eat very much solid food. He glanced out sparingly, confident in his camouflage but taking few chances.

Of course they were out there, spooks behind every tree, in boats, in the air. The breaking waves trickled cool splashes over the blind, a natural shield against infrared. No one would walk the break wall. Nor could they, it was far too tragic. Optics were their only defense. Spatz need only hide and bide his time. They might find the blind, but by the time ballistics reconstructed the scene and pinpointed the angle, he would be long, long gone.

The mayor sucked up his faux praise. As a headliner himself, he might draw a few hundred, tops, but as an opening act, he was able to proclaim to thousands. Trust didn't wait for the introduction, he was famously impatient and had enough of listening to the lessor evil speak. The mayor was caught off-guard when the crowd suddenly roared, thinking for the briefest of moments they cheered for him.

Until then, the mayor never knew how gratifying it was, how great he must be, how catchy and eloquent his words must have just been. The look on his face upon realization of his error left a permanent and embarrassing scar that he spent the rest of his political career trying to conceal with hate for Trust.

"Patriots unite!" Trust shook his hands over his head as if he had just won it all.

The people didn't come for an explanation that day, because whatever plastic words Trust strung together to excuse the post were going to be more than strong enough for those who were light on concept to stand upon.

This crowd really came to pray, they just didn't know it. If God's fans were half as excited, the world would burn to the ground.

"Ladies and gentlemen, I stand before you today to tell you unequivocally, I was hacked!" The crowd exploded with satisfaction.

"Do not believe the lies of the left! They hate you! They hate me! Why would they ever tell you the truth? It's very sad actually, very sad. Today I pledge to you that we will spare no expense to get to the bottom of this, this falsehood, this attack on decency. These..."

It was an incredibly brief moment, and the footage has to be slowed all the way down in order to see it, but as he was speaking, many, including some lip-reading experts have said the word that was about to leave his mouth started with a "B" and ended with "astards".

Unfortunately for Trust, in order for that to have taken place, he was going to need better access to air. It is a person's breath traveling out of their body and over their vocal chords which makes sound. Once the bullet passed through his heart, velocity removed breathing from the equation, and alas, the word was never officially spoken.

Center, why wouldn't it be?

• • •

"Hello my friend," the voice said.

"Who is that? Where am I? How did I get here?" Trust asked.

"Whoa, whoa, slow down. Let's start with who. My name is Baron Samedi, and you may call me either Baron, or Samedi, it does not matter to me. However, if you call me both I might think you too serious and who knows if I trust you after that?" The Baron laughed.

"Yeah but where…" Trust stammered.

"Enough! You don't talk now. I talk now. You are in between time and there is not a moment to spare. Think of that while you hear me. Look, that is you, right there."

Trust was shown a view of himself one second after the bullet's impact. Others on stage were still actively trying to catch his falling corpse.

"You are on your way somewhere my friend and I am not talking about that body and the ground. I do not normally do this but for you, I make a special deal. Think about it, too bad you did not live through this one. To people you would be invincible. You would get every vote, everywhere man," Samedi said.

"What? I…I can't believe, I wish…" Trust stuttered from the shock of what he was seeing.

"Then wish no more man. Samedi can make it happen. It's just paper man, after all," Samedi laughed harder.

"What? Make what happen?" Trust asked.

"For the sake of all man, what you out there for? You gonna be president some day! Big man, all that! You gonna fix the world remember? Make everything great again!" Samedi said.

"They shot me, they actually did it. But how am I here? How am I seeing this? Who did this to me?"

"Never mind all that now man. It don't matter no more. Nothing you can do from here, nothing that is unless you take the deal," Samedi said.

"Deal? What deal?" Trust asked.

"You do not listen to me. I make you live man, and then you get to be president, otherwise you die here, and you go," he said.

"Go? Go where?" Trust asked.

Samedi belly laughed. "No, no, no, you probably should not get your hopes up rich man," he chided.

"Ok, so what do I have to do?" Trust asked.

Samedi leaned in close at an odd angle, head cocked hard to one side while keeping his chin further back. The effect was a shadow over his face below his nose accentuating the white of his teeth. He waved his finger in Trust's face, a universal 'no' that left Trust confused.

"You so willing. You do anything to live. To get them that got you huh?" Samedi asked.

Trust did not immediately answer. Instead he took his time to stare at his own body frozen in time, dying.

"What is it that you want? What could a man give you?" Trust asked.

"Life man!" Samedi laughed. "You gotta keep the people from dying. No wars, no drugs, help them up when they need help," he said.

Trust again stayed silent.

"What? Not what you expected? This a good thing man. What you think?" Samedi said.

"You know what I think? I think you're playing me, I think a lot of people are going to die," Trust said.

The Baron scoffed at Trust's reply. It angered him.

"Pfft, a lot of people always die. Who cares? They all gonna die anyways. You gonna die my friend, just not today. The secret is what happen after. They get them. You think you got power? You think I got power? Hahahaha. That's not the real power man, the real power lies beyond what you know, what you can think of, and it is dark now, cause the people gone dark. So much hate, they angry at everything. You and your kind make it that way," Samedi was purposeful and sinister.

"I'm not sure I understand how this helps you," Trust said.

"You rather die than make a bad deal? I know this about you. Okay. I say to you it is the desperate who keep Samedi powerful. Your life is all you got, all you ever gonna have. Nothing else you got mean anything to me. Today, you get to live. But someday, I might ask you for more. Who knows? On that day, you get to decide again but until that day come, once you Mr. President, you gonna be that forever," Samedi said.

"What about pain? I'm not a big fan of…"

"Enough! Time is up, I am done with you! Say yes or you go in 3, 2, …"

"He's alive!" one of the men working on Trust screamed. Rescuers who were sure he was dead seconds earlier went from dread and reckoning to lighting the spire of hope as they worked with renewed vigor and diligence to save their hero.

"It's a miracle! He's alive!" they screamed in joy.

The scene was mired in chaos as the machine kicked into gear. A landing zone was quickly cordoned off for the ambulatory helicopter. Law enforcement of every ilk flew around like bees.

"I think it came from over there. No, it came from up there. There was two shots at least. The government did it," witnesses fought at the expense of answers.

Protestors swung their signs and banners of discontent like freedom flags, delivered from evil by evil, while over-filled pots of sycophants boiled over and spread the flames. People on both sides were beaten and stabbed with whatever was available. Police were overwhelmed and they themselves became victims as well as perpetrators of the violence which spread across the country.

The media blackout from the Trust campaign was only making matters worse. The ICU treating him was swarmed with reporters from around the world. Satellite dishes, police batons, and prayer candles mixed flawlessly into a madman's salad of bedlam.

Conspiracy theories rose from the ashes. Most say he was killed, and the rumors of his survival were the only thing staving off civil war. Some proclaimed the end of days, and his death was merely retribution from God, and so they prayed. Some thanked God for

Trust's untimely demise, so they prayed. And then there were those who held hope that he was alive, that he would pull through and lead them to salvation, so they prayed.

The heads up was one hour, one hour until the press conference to be held in front of the main entrance to the hospital. The campaign had one contingent for delivering the information, silence. No questions allowed and keep the clicks to a minimum.

Exactly on time Press Secretary Kelly McGinnis stepped out of the hospital and up to an incredible bank of microphones. His body language screamed bad news as the nation held its breath.

"Ladies and gentlemen, thank you for coming. Thank you America for your thoughts and prayers during these tumultuous times. They are in fact, making a difference. May I please direct your attention to the screen to my left."

Trust was smiling, even waving, although he was clearly not strong enough to lift his arm off the hospital bed. He was surrounded by electronics and tubes, none of which were currently attached to his body besides an IV. There was what would be described later as a worldwide collective hush, and then he spoke.

"That what doesn't kill us, only makes us stronger. It was a miracle I survived. They shot me in the heart but I'm stronger than they know. We are stronger than they know. Thank you for the love, see you soon."

With a half smile and weak wave the screen went dark. McGinnis immediately retreated to the higher ground back through the front doors, safe from the tsunami of reporters crashing the podium with an aggregate white noise of questions and demands.

Chapter Twenty-two

Pride Cometh

"Half the world is gonna hate me. The other half? Too bad they'll never know," Spatz said to himself before pulling on his mask and sliding out through the bottom of the blind.

Ever since he got there, Spatz has been cleaning away any evidence of his existence, packing everything out and wiping the entirety of the inside surface. He knew there wouldn't be time for dilly-dallying after he took the shot.

Chaos was expected but, more than that, he was counting on it to help mask his getaway. He swam slowly and close to the bottom. He used a rebreather which absorbs the carbon dioxide of the user's exhaled breath and recycles the unused oxygen, adding more when needed. A rebreather also extends dive time and eliminates the bubble trail on the surface. Not that anyone would notice with the coast guard dinghies zig-zagging haphazardly to and fro.

He pushed the rifle into the silty bottom of the lake before he swam through the harbor and up the river to where his boat was slipped. Whatever else he had, mostly clothing, he left to the currents, eventually destined for the deep water of the lake. If it could float, it wasn't invited on the mission.

Under his boat he stashed his dive gear in a large mesh bag tied off just below the surface to one of the pilings. Wearing only swim trunks he pulled himself into a tiny rubber dinghy tied to the main boat comfortably out of sight under the pier.

Inside the raft he had cleaning supplies and an assortment of vinyl graphics so that he could seamlessly transition to the act of applying them to the hull, a job that had already begun days earlier on the starboard side.

Spatz had gone to great lengths to avoid getting caught and although his level of self-satisfaction was high, he felt empty. The pinnacle of his career, the most important shot he'll probably ever take, and he wouldn't even be a footnote in history.

"Hell, you were more loved than I'll ever be," he said.

A doll floated face down past his slip, spinning in the back current of the pilings. She had been in the water for some time, evident by the scum line on her exposed plastic skin and the ultraviolet destruction of every part not under water. He nearly fished her out but decided her company probably wasn't worth the effort. He already said everything he wanted to say.

• • •

"Trust is never given, it is earned, and my fellow Americans, I think we can all agree, that he has earned every bit of his name," the crowd went wild.

Enter Orquidea Ciego, esteemed district 28 Congresswoman from the great state of Florida. Paying too much attention to her name or the tone of her skin was considered pandering, which was off the table quicker than the venerable meatball. No one dare say the quiet part out loud. Nothing could be more American than the daughter of an undocumented immigrant rising to one of the most powerful political positions in the world. One Muerte premature from giving her the power to hold her elaborately painted nail over the button.

She was highly applauded, both locally and nationally, as being a champion for immigration, both legal and otherwise, a fact that did not sit well with some of the Trusted. For them, her ability to help them win trumped such fears like constipation from painkillers.

Normally, the candidate, typically a headliner, announces a running mate at the party convention earlier in the calendar year of the election. In this cycle, everything was different. All the rules went out the window after "The Attempt". With Trust simply not well enough to pound the campaign trail, and nearly three months till the RNC convention, he needed a general to carry his flag.

Ciego brought controversy to every crowd and mic. She draped herself in the flag. It was her figurative cape, her cloak, her sail. She practically branded it.

Red, white, and Trust Ciego were close range shotgun splattered on everything from coffee mugs to prophylactics. They painted "The Attempt" as being right up there with 9/11, Pearl Harbor, and the Great Depression. It was timeline defining, a notch in everybody's life post- and pre-, a marketing bloodbath sparing no one whether they had to shit or go blind.

Meanwhile Americanism was being held up as a sickness, a disease sneezed into the fan by right wing zealots who according to some were over-loving their country to the demise of civilization itself. The left only begrudgingly accepted the fact that red and blue did in fact also exist in the rainbow.

• • •

"I am, doll parts, bad skin, doll heart," the words played over and over in his head as he floated face down in the river.

He was happy, maybe even a little loopy after laying on the bottom for days. It took years of practice before he was able to consistently fall tails down. He could land face up most of the time, especially if he had a little warning.

• • •

If Tyler Hansen had one weakness besides being eternally shy, afraid of anything and everything outside his door, and hygiene, it would be marijuana. Reefer, cannabis, the Devil's lettuce, whatever the popular vernacular of the day, didn't matter. It was the only way he would leave his house, high. Under the guise of fight fire with fire, Tyler countered real, earned paranoia with a synthetic alternative.

In high school, Tyler's athleticism peaked on a skateboard that has rolled down an aging ramp ever since. A trip to the corner store for rolling papers was a cash endeavor as there was no way he would ever take the risk of being found with a debit or credit card.

Occasionally, when a person is high, their dexterity is less than what they commonly enjoy when sober. Today was that day for Tyler Hansen, the day he lost a very important coin, his "guardian angel" as it fell unknown at the time out of his pocket and onto a broken blacktop parking lot in the rain, face down.

"Seriously? You lost him? When and where? Don't move, I'll be right there," Ms. Maximine said heatedly.

The coin barely had a chance to get wet before he was scooped up and slid into the dark canvas front pocket of a local fisherman. There he blended with other coins of varied value, none sentient. He was blind inside and deafened by the jingle.

It didn't take Sherlock Holmes to start with the video monitoring equipment of the convenience store where the coin was lost but it did take a little longer to find out where he slipped his boat. It was well after midnight before Philippine caught up with him and in any other world other than hers, the recovery may have been completely benign. That is until a man dressed in a black frog suit with matching gun case very carefully and quietly slid into the water amidst the shadows of his boat in the wee hours of the morning immediately after flipping the coin overboard.

Sherlock also had no part in taking the first step on the ladder labeled "VIP Visitor" and getting a better view of the park. The next step, post shooting took her to an empty salmon boat slipped a short distance upriver from the harbor park and consequently to the top of the ladder. Up there it had another label that said "Danger, do not stand or sit", so she made herself a cup of coffee, set it down on top and waited.

"Nice job sailor, where's the gun? I know where one is," she said.

Ms. Maximine was leaning over the gunwale, gently tapping her pistol on the stainless railing smiling down on Spatz in his dinghy, whose heart may as well have stopped on the spot.

"Gun? What gun?" he looked down at the water anticipating an aquatic escape.

"It's gonna hurt," she said raising her pistol.

By the time he raised his hands authorities were closing in from every angle. Land, sea, and air. Even if he could get to his gear below and managed to get it on without drowning, government frog men perched on black inflatables would have apprehended him with time to spare.

Ms. Maximine shrunk from the opportunity to be a national hero, instead choosing the anonymity granted by her former position. The government had little in the form of evidence as long as Spatz chose the fifth and they knew as much. However, a hurdle this size never bothered them before. He would be held indefinitely in the interest of national defense until such evidence could be either found or manufactured.

• • •

As for Skeleton Man, once the waves set him upright, he entered a patriotic teddy bear before being forced to wear Trust's face on four billboards, a syrup lady on a bus and two different cabby ID's before he could find his way back to the office. He always found a way home.

● ● ●

Spatz came to in a concrete room, walls, ceiling, and floor that pitched to the center focus of a cast iron drain about the size of a grapefruit. The lighting was dim at best, provided by two recessed lights with yellow bulbs covered by thick plexiglass. He laid on the floor next to a heavy, not very wide wooden bench the length of a tall man.

The door was gray steel with no visible latch and a thousand coats of paint working together to hide the rust below. It's repeated swing left a rust trail on the floor mapping its way to a pile of wet moldy rags.

They came in practiced, lightning fast, six men, some carrying things they dropped once inside.

"It all happened so fast," Spatz would recall.

They picked him up and slammed him onto the bench, back down, and strapped him into place. Safely contained, the seventh and eighth men came into the room and closed the door behind them.

"Good afternoon Mr. Clarke," Mr. Carlito said. "Before we get underway, I'm going to give you a chance to give me the details," Carl explained.

"Details to what? Who are you people?" Spatz demanded.

"I would like to introduce you to my associate, Eric Jon. He and his team are here to help you in one of the most common and worst possible ways to remember. Gentlemen," Mr. Carl knocked twice, the door opened and he left.

"Wait, wait, this is bullshit! This isn't legal," Spatz screamed.

The surge of moldy, cold, damp and musty took his breath away as what he assumed was one of the towels from the corner was pulled tight over his face. The bench tipped back, elevating his feet and water was poured over the towel.

Spatz was no fool, he knew before they did it that he was about to be water-boarded, but that didn't help. At some point, once both flight and fight are definitively removed from the equation, fear takes over and the brain betrays you because as far as Spatz was concerned, he was drowning.

Eric Jon came into Carlito's office drenched in *I told you so* satisfaction.

"Did he give us what we wanted?" Mr. Carlito asked.

"He did, everything. We have boots on the ground now, live feed," Jon said.

"By all means," Carl said motioning to the monitor on his office wall.

They were able to witness in real time the approach to the break-wall. Men hopped and climbed until one misconstrued jump accidentally revealed the tell-tale hollow thump of non-stone.

"Who knows?" Mr. Carlito asked.

"You, me, our team, the woman, the lawyer. Well, she knows someone has him, she just doesn't know it's us," Jon said.

"Good, let's keep it that way. Get him in the program, I fuckin' love this guy," Mr. Carl said.

"And what if he says no? Fame? Prison?" Jon asked.

"No, I don't think so. Let him know the target lived then show him just exactly what it is that we do here, what it's like to be wiped out, to have never existed. Pride cometh before the fall, show him the fall."

"The Press?" Jon asked.

"Let me worry about the optics. He wasn't the guy, Maximine was wrong, apprehended an innocent man. Perfect, sink her ass too. Two birds with one stone."

Chapter Twenty-three

Tuesdays Gone with a Win

Election day, every candidate is the best, and the worst, ever. Doomsayers insist that the country will never recover while optimistic opposers preach that the future remains blinding bright. For either, the economy would boom through the financial crash of a generation depending on who held the scepter. People shaped like paper ballots stacked a mile high will carve a new face on a figurehead who at any moment may have the country teetering on the edge of war or one thousand years of peace, whichever is worse.

The newest and most important aspect of the day is determining who cheated. It's guaranteed, a locked down solid easy bet, free money that whichever side loses accuses the other of stealing the election. Of course there's cheating, and then there's cheating. A player would argue that not telling your little sister you landed on Saint James Place and skipping out on fourteen dollars in rent is a hell of a lot different than sliding stolen yellow five hundred dollar bills under the board. The latter move having a much higher potential of proving that cheaters do in fact win and prosper.

Trust was out and about flaunting a near miraculous rate of healing. If his age were ever in question, slamming death's door closed with both hands and his dick, which was very much in question, rendered the argument moot. He had emotion at the wheel racing downhill with its foot to the floor while he shouted "go, go" from the seat behind. He stared through tinted glass at the other car he considered autonomous, a robot without feeling or love of country and quite possibly, piloted by someone else entirely.

The Trusted dubbed him 3PO, a shiny robot who spoke every language but didn't understand people. The world called him Hohlen, Peter Hohlen, deniable President of The United States.

Hohlen entered the office through the left door. People say if he had the flu and the bathroom was on the right, he'd sooner make on the carpet. The weight of his administration over time compressed the oval office, sinking the floor on the left, raising it on the right. Marbles and syncopates rolled down hill and routinely found themselves stuck against the wall.

The outcome was anybody's guess. Predictability pollsters were an old woman drenched in patchouli glaring out from under a fake eye patch dealing tarot from a wood spoked carnival trailer. By late afternoon, exits showed Hohlen with a solid lead which caused a segment to slow down and accidentally improve the quality of their protest signs.

By dinner time for all but the early birds, the race tightened up, a prime-time match-up made to order for networks and political junkies. Strongholds were called as predicted and bellwether counties lied to their spouses about where they spent last night.

After the polls closed, 'too close to call' became a universal rallying cry. Percentages meant little compared to the actual numbers of votes needed because at their core people were just plain lazy. The boxes were heavy and nobody wanted to have to load up and haul more ballots than necessary.

"How are we doing today Mr. Jon?" Carlito asked.

He came in early that day, way before the polls opened. As far as he was concerned, voting never made much sense when the outcome was already decided.

"Cyber is wild today, we're shutting down anybody who might have any influence at all but we're letting the big boys run to avoid any suspicion," Jon replied.

"Excellent. And the machines?" Carl asked.

"Straight and narrow at the moment. We'd rather not get inside if we don't have to. That's the first place people who don't understand how ass wipe works will look for blame, and then we're going to have to make smart people lie, and that sort of thing is almost always obvious," Jon said.

"No matter, they'll believe what we tell them, eventually. It's not like they'll have a choice. Let's just keep our eyes on everything. Any trends, things out of the ordinary. As usual, if someone is making too much noise, handle them, especially today. Let's let the paper boys do their thing if we need them. Today is the one day of the year when paper beats the hell out of scissors, every time," Carl quipped.

• • •

There were dozens, maybe more, mostly men but not exclusively. They found themselves existing nearly suddenly in the afternoon sunlight next to a small, shaded stream. Bird song filled the air only making more noticeable the random buzz of passing flies. Wildflowers from a nearby meadow diluted the scent of mud drying on the banks. It was warm there, a feeling none of them had enjoyed for quite some time.

Wherever they came from, they came slowly, so slow as to appear not to be moving at all. They were semi-transparent, not yet of proper mass to reflect the light of the living. They were confused as they were used to near total blackness, existing in a place or universe that only allowed the dimmest of light. The occasional sighting of another would only serve to remind them that they were still conscious.

They all had two things in common. First, they each possessed a certain skill that he required. Second, they all made a deal with Samedi and consequently have existed as his trapped souls ever since their deaths.

The creek was only inches deep, babbling crystal clear over round colorful stones. He came sauntering, nearly dancing down the middle. He gazed at the water smiling, marveling at the wildlife around him. He placed his cane near the shoreline and held it still for a small green frog to jump aboard. He released it on the other side as hungry trout looked on from just below the surface. Baron Samedi's hardy laugh filled the air as he raised his arms in typical showman fashion.

"Hello my children! Isn't this beautiful? Ha, ha, you my friends are not used to such a place. This is the deal you made. But today? Today is your lucky day. Today I give you a new deal, and then you get to go home."

"But first you gotta do for me one thing. Each of you, one thing. I will take you to a place, I will give you flesh, hahaha, but not for long. You feel it even now, the weight of life, the color of seeing with eyes. Use your skills, as I am and move on, or choose not to and be in the blackness for all time, no hope," Samedi explained.

He walked among them, looking into each set of eyes as they began to appear nearly solid, wearing whatever clothes they used to think they wore. Although still barely noticeable, it became apparent that they could also move. One by one they disappeared with Samedi.

Samedi and the first taken soul, stood in an alley behind a high rise apartment building. They hid in the shadow of an overflowing dumpster, in the earliest hours of the morning. They watched a man hurriedly loading boxes off of a handcart into the trunk of his car.

"You remember how she sounded? How you felt that day? She screamed so much, so much pain. Burned alive in her car? So much hate man. Samedi got you outta that one huh? Now, you burn this one, same way, all of it, all of him. Then Samedi talk to him. And you? You go free man. Now go, go now and do what you do!" Samedi demanded.

The first taken struck the man across the side of his face with a broken brick. His upper body collapsed into the trunk where the process was repeated over and again until it was abundantly clear that the man would no longer be moving. The first taken then entered the car and ripped off a plastic access panel under the dashboard. Immediately the wires were smoking and only moments later engulfed in total fire.

He stood next to the car and stared back at Samedi who could barely be seen nodding his approval in the deepest corner of the shadow. By the time people arrived, the car was an unapproachable firestorm of black smoke and noxious fumes and the first taken faded out of existence along with tens of thousands of ballots.

Thousand to one type incidents bordering on horrific were happening around the country and all within a short window. A safe in Pennsylvania that would weigh well over a thousand pounds was found on top of its unfortunate owner, crushing his life away. A handful of miscellaneous ballots were found at the scene. First shifters at a warehouse in Milwaukee, forcibly entered in the night, found a shift guard impaled on a forklift, the delivery van stolen. Days later while investigating the cause of a broken guardrail on the river front, the van was found on the bottom in twenty feet of water, packed with illegibly wet ballots.

The list went on and on, bodies were turning up everywhere throughout the night without a suspect in sight. One by one, Samedi set his tortured souls free, replacing them with fresh fools who almost always had one last wish before they died.

• • •

"Yeah? Jon, it's the middle of the night. No, no. What happened, where are they? What? Yeah, yeah, I'll be right there," Mr. Carl said hanging up the phone.

Mr. Carlito and Eric Jon stood in the office blankly staring at the many screens on the wall trying to figure out what was happening.

"Who's doing this? This is top end, nothing small about it. The machines, what about the machines?" Carl asked.

"It's too late, we figured the paper boys would make the delivery. Everything was all set, in place. Almost every single one was intercepted. The ones who made it didn't have enough to make a difference. Looking at the numbers, I'd say we're fucked," Jon said.

"No! We have got to find out who is responsible for this. There had to be a leak, something. They fuck with me they will pay, guaranteed," Carl threatened.

"And if it's him? I mean, it was clearly someone. Like you said, top end," Jon said.

"Oh, he'll pay too. Nobody is beyond our reach. Nobody," Mr. Carl said.

• • •

Trust and his team were holding vigil in a luxury suite in downtown Manhattan. They were hooked into every exit poll imaginable, every news agency. They had eyes, ears, and boots on the ground across the country. In the early morning hours, they were cautiously optimistic.

A trusted executive assistant who had been with the campaign from the very beginning entered the war room. She was physically and emotionally destroyed, keeping herself alive on caffeine, sugar, and the occasional shot of whiskey.

"Excuse me, Mr. Trust. Um, I…'"

"Well go ahead, spit it out," Trust said impatiently.

"Well, I normally wouldn't do this but there is a little girl here. Like a scout or something," she said pointing behind her with both hands.

"At this hour? Is she alone?" Trust asked.

"Yes, I just, I should have sent her away but for some reason, I don't know, I have to you know, come get you," she explained.

"What does she want?" a different staffer asked.

"She said she needs to see you. It's urgent. Her exact words were, 'Trust me, when he sees me, he'll know exactly why I'm here,'" she said.

Intrigued, Trust stepped out to meet the little girl. There, in the foyer, among security and other staffers, who all under oath would swear were standing next to a little girl, stood Samedi, smiling, holding a scout bag.

"I brought you something Mr. Trust," Samedi said.

Only Trust could see him and he immediately played along.

"Oh, hello. Yes, yes of course, gentlemen let her in. Right this way, finally, the cookies I wanted," Trust said guiding her to the main room of the suite.

"Kinda public hey man?" Samedi said quietly.

"I can't very well take you into a bedroom looking like that now can I?" Trust said.

"No matter, I make it short. You gonna win man, no question," Samedi said as people gathered around.

"Excuse me? A little space please," Trust protested to the room.

"I don't understand. How do you know? The numbers aren't all in yet," Trust said.

"Oh they in, they lookin' for more but they ain't gonna find any," Samedi giggled like a little girl.

"Thank you Mr. Trust, sir! You're the bestest ever! Here's your cookies!" Samedi said loudly as he handed Trust a box, gave him a huge hug and walked to the door wearing a ridiculous smile.

Samedi stopped just short of walking through.

"Quick Mr. President rock, paper…" he pumped his little girl arm forward and formed the universal game sign of paper. Trust put out scissors.

"Hahahaha! Not today Mr. President, not today," Samedi said laughing on his way out.

Chapter Twenty-four

Dislike

Conspiracies are much like tires, if they have proper traction, they can in most circumstances find their way through the deep mud. Of course this is assuming the drive train is up to the task. Even if they are hopelessly sunk, a little bit of tread showing is all it takes to breed hope, so they spin.

The grassy knoll, the moon landings, crashed flying saucers, and most recently, stolen elections. Part of the recipe for a solid theory is the ever looming question of authenticity. The questions of *did they really happen?* or *are they faked?* are essential ingredients. Too clear of an answer deflates the tires.

Whether the synchrony was fate or circumstance is up for debate, but the election did coincide with a new and wholly terrorizing malady. It was at the time unknown to science. As a matter of fact, science could not determine one way or another if a person who suffered from it had anything wrong with them, at all.

Doctors and scientists scoured the neurological cupboards and could not find a thing to eat. There existed zero chemical imbalances besides what was already known or expected. Physically people were unaffected besides the onset of atrophy. No viruses, bacteria strain, or parasites were prevalent.

Possibly most baffling was the initial distribution. It had no rhyme or reason, popping up simultaneously across the globe. Unlike the great flus of years past, this one seemed to ignore the poor, and it was spreading.

It was known to come on rather suddenly, in most cases, a matter of minutes. A person could be fine, and seconds later they became the simplest of fools, incapable of any decisions. They couldn't even help but randomly soil themselves, and speaking was out of the question. Often when they would haplessly wander and fall, they would stay down to rest, existing merely on the instinct of a plant.

It was dubbed Severe Onset Catatonia but unlike the standard existing medically accepted definition of a catatonic state, medication had no effect. Some blamed vapor contrails, calling them chemtrails and worked tirelessly to convince the world that airplanes were spreading chemicals to thin the population, or make it sterile, or dumb it down, or whatever. Some blamed processed foods, arguing genetically modified organisms were being used for all the same reasons. Hardly anyone blamed The Troll Hunters at first, but that theory was definitely starting to gain traction.

"It was the government" was trending out of the box as many believed that it was the only entity capable of pulling it all off. The sickness did seem to have an adverse effect on leftist voters for reasons that remained a mystery. The issue with this particular theory is the government in charge at the time, Hohlen's government, would hardly cut its own throat, much less its head completely off.

The fear of the disease was also said to have kept people away from the polls although the pavement was dry on the topic until after the election. Many took to wearing masks in public without any idea if transmission through the air was even a possibility. A better-safe-than-sorry mentality took over and those who did not comply were labeled monsters who did not care about their fellow humans. When people in masks were affected, proponents of the practice falsely claimed they must have been infected before they even put them on.

Through it all, the internet was on fire. It was now the primary source of news and information for most people under sixty years of age. And those over that mark had their lives affected by it whether they knew it or not.

On most platforms, Troll Hunters was quickly becoming the loudest whisper in the theatre. Big name influencers were falling by the wayside, some victims of the virus, others deniably targeted by the company.

Their many followers, those who saw what they posted, listened to what they said, were now spread thin among the masses. A redistribution of influence caused accurate information to be more difficult to locate. The squeakiest wheel no longer got the grease, it was now the most interesting wheel that garnered all the attention. Decisions about who or what to notice were collectively and accidentally made by the masses who were in control and didn't even know it.

And it was collectively, if not mass anecdotally that they discovered those who caught it, the virus, were by all accounts actively engaged online. Also, as far as anyone could remember, there had never been a company like Troll Hunters. A company that advertised online a service that would take others offline, or make them disappear forever, or maybe turn them into zombies. The latter two of course not quite appearing in the fine print of the contract. It was guilt by memes and clicks, an unenforceable verdict rendered by a majority who had nothing better to do with their time.

Imagine Daniel Navarro's surprise when someone actually exercised decorum and knocked on his office door.

"Yes?" Daniel asked.

Mr. Carlito came in quickly toting a suspiciously positive attitude.

"Good morning Mr. President. I just wanted to take some time to stop by and say, hey, how've things been going lately? I've been pretty busy, haven't really had the time to stop and see how you've, well, let's say, adapted to the roll so to speak," he said.

"Fine, fine, face of the company and all that. Although now that you mention it, not that you care, but the buzz isn't good. People are starting to think we're responsible for the virus. I mean. All that other stuff, I guess that's your department, but the other thing…" Daniel paused.

"Honestly that's one of the things I wanted to talk to you about. Like I said, been busy, too busy as a matter of fact. With this virus, and like you said, other things, it has been suggested that I take a step back, maybe take a less active role in management. That of course puts you squarely back in the driver's seat. Don't get me wrong, the structure we have in place remains, you just won't be hearing from, or seeing me nearly as often," Carl said.

"How often then?" Daniel asked.

"Well, never," Carl said.

"What? Never?"

"Yes, once I leave those doors you will most likely never see me again," Carl said.

"Who's the next Mr. Carlito? The next guy I have to answer to?" Daniel asked.

"TBD, to be determined. In the meantime, you have the reigns. I bid you good day sir," Carl said leaving just as quickly as he came in.

"Hey! Wait, wait! What about? Hey!" Daniel yelled.

Smashing his wrists into the wheels of his chair he made for the door as fast as he could but to no avail, Carlito was long gone.

"You gotta be fucking kidding me," he said to his former secretary who stealthily returned to her desk outside his office door. A post she was forced to vacate due to the recently defunct management.

● ● ●

People love to dislike things. Ask an introvert at a party what he likes to do with his free time and you'll be squeezing the answer from a dry orange. Ask him what he doesn't like about being there and you'll have to excuse yourself to get another drink.

For Trust, it was time to officially gloat. He won decisively and he could hardly wait to shake his own hands over his head and thank himself for the victory in front of the world. He assembled his campaign staff.

"Thanks for coming team. Great job, and I mean a great job one and all. This is big. Really, really big. How about a round of applause for everyone here," Trust said.

"But, but it's just the beginning friends, only the beginning. Let's get out there with the best acceptance speech ever, of all time. I want primetime, I want cable, hell, I want the internet. Let's get the internet, the whole damn thing. Hundreds of millions of people, everybody should see us, hear us. Let's get it out there! Great job again, let's do this!" Trust said amongst the applause.

The team returned to stuffing their honeycombs, while Trust and a chosen few retired to his office. One hour after lunch eastern time and everything was set in stone, although Hohlen had yet to officially concede. His campaign was far too busy perpetuating perceived fraud but what they really wanted to know was who took the yellow five hundred dollar bills they had stashed under the board.

It was a live event from Madison Square Garden, held inside where the secret service would now be forced to step up their protection of Trust. The podium was nearly completely obscured by a blooming flower of microphones.

As opening speaker, Director McGillis' pleasantries were the strike of a wooden match against the people who were hot wicks, burning fast. The hiss of the powder were the words they waited for, "Ladies and gentlemen, the next president of the United States…" and boom!

Everybody wanted a slice of the pie, networks, internet channels, advertisers, but it was the social media platform companies who stood to benefit the most. They weren't just going to broadcast a blurb from grandma's favorite pro bowling channel, they were going to reach out and touch the whole world, without commercials, without interruption.

Showing its prowess as the platform with the greatest perceived level of sophistication, the most popular app amongst all the social networks decided to change its game if only slightly. One simple addition would allow them to track their audience more accurately than ever before. One little feature they never had before, released specifically for this event, a dislike button.

And so they pressed, over and over again. As unhappy faces flew up like balloons randomly across their screens, opponents sent hordes of happy emojis to counter. A silent war waged, fought by cartoon faces in the minds of people who cared more about the numbers of smiles and frowns than they did for soldiers who died fighting political wars in real life.

Apocalyptic anger and vitriol bruised the fingertips of Trust haters pounding dents into their glass screens with aggressive dislikes.

It was everything he needed, The Hunter. It was more than he could have ever hoped for. So much negativity, so much contact. He felt them all, welcomed them as he opened up the gates and took them all in at once.

So many phones hit the ground at one time that it was actually recorded on Richter scales as a slight tremor felt around the world. Estimates were off the charts with some saying that the virus had taken as many as a hundred million globally, in an instant. The Trusted called it nothing but a conspiracy.

The live crowd comprised of mostly sycophants was largely unaffected. Trust, busy pounding like Adolph on the tablet from where he read his speech was forced to take a step back.

The life drained from his eyes as he squinted, but just a bit as if he were angry. He gripped the podium with both hands and ceased to speak. The crowd cheered louder, expecting a memorable moment or line, maybe a grand finale, but there was nothing.

Trust pushed the top-heavy podium flush with microphones violently sending it summersaulting into the crowd. He was overcome with anger without reason. Staffers rushed him to pull him off stage but he was stronger than they would have ever guessed. At the bottom of a people pile Trust gouged out the left eye of a woman he had known and loved for over twenty years.

Proponents would say he was attacked, possibly chemically, like so many others who would become victims that day. However, for unknown reasons, including but not limited to his inert qualities of strength and leadership, Trust was spared from catatonia. This was nothing more than a half truth that ignored what he had really become, enraged, irritable, and physically stronger. He also possessed a sudden and complete lack of reason, patience, or empathy.

"It's, it's like, I don't know, like he ate a bowl of instant evil or something. I don't know what happened," McGillis said to the staff during an update.

If a landscape picture had only two eyes taking up the entire frame they would have belonged to Samedi, scared awake. They would have been bright white against a true black background and would have gone bloodshot red with a quickness.

"I do, I know, and I know who. And that means I'm comin' for you," Samedi sang to himself in a tune he only just made up on the spot.

Chapter Twenty-five

You're Hired

"And we was gonna be such good friends too…"

Samedi's dire message boomed through the darkness of the Hunter's world with too much bass, a PA system run amok in an empty stadium.

"Promising them freedom, while they themselves are slaves of corruption; for by what a man is overcome, by this he is enslaved," The Hunter said.

"Do not quote scripture to me boy! I am no man! I am a god!" Samedi yelled, angry.

He appeared in the darkness as a giant, smiling down on the Hunter, strolling around in boots long as cars and tall as a house.

"Seems like a man is too big lately. Maybe it's time for Samedi to step on him, hard." The Baron slammed his foot down and spun it into metaphorical dirt.

Without so much as acknowledging what Samedi had done, the Hunter vanished.

"I see you play games. Yes, sure, games, of course, hahaha. What better place?" Samedi joked. "But you go too far my friend. You should not have taken him. He was mine," he slammed his foot down angrily.

"Samedi warn you, long ago, do not take the ones whose bad thoughts make them happy. I told you who they belong to, I tell you they got a power. And now look what you have done? Look at all the souls. The minds gonna notice now, gonna come looking," Samedi explained.

"Another deal?" The Hunter asked.

It was the Hunter's voice that surrounded now, and Samedi looked pleased.

"He's mine now, they all are," The Hunter said.

"Enough! I will see you now," Samedi yelled.

The Baron spun his cane around over his head in grand sweeping motions. Light of every color sprayed from the tip and landed as white upon the ground until all the world he was in was covered with brightness. All besides one speck, a singularity, an optical illusion, a black fly on a movie screen at a distance difficult to judge.

"There, you cannot hide from Samedi," he said pointing his cane at the tiny anomaly.

It was then that the speck began to move, slowly at first but progressively faster. It circled Samedi, over him, under him, drawing a pencil trail in its wake exponentially accelerating on each pass until only the slightest sliver of white remained.

The Baron lunged for the sliver of light, digging his nails in on either side of it, barely holding onto the edge of the darkness he pulled with all his might. The black turned to tar in his hands and he fell backwards as it closed in around him. Furious he once again took to swinging his cane to reintroduce light but before the first revolution it banged hard into something metal and immobile. The report was a deafening resonance from an unseen bell and it cracked the cane askew in his hand. As he drew it close to assess the damage it turned into a black and white serpent without end that thoroughly wrapped and choked him.

The next singularity had hints of green and blue and he rushed towards it as fast as he could ever remember moving under his own power or the influence of others. It grew larger of course as he neared and within a moment he was free of the snake along a lakeside in the sun, where the water clapped gently against a sandy shoreline.

The Hunter sat close by, perched comfortably on an easy chair sized boulder, one leg stretched out on top while the other dangled and tickled the surface of the water.

The Hunter said, "You're just like the rest, use, destroy, waste. I am fair and always have been. I killed fairly and let live fairly. I thought I might owe you a pleasantry for giving this all to me. I thought you gave me time, an eternity, access and control of a world that I have always needed but that was never true was it?"

"You did not die. You did not kill me. I did these things, I brought myself here, through my actions, through my witness and testimony to what humans are, what they can be. You know what they really are? They're parasites, like you. You are nothing more than a politician. You are no God, you are just old. Old mud washed off the boots of creators and you didn't even have the courtesy to take your place in line, in the filthy swirl on your way down the drain."

"They are mine, all of them, even the one you warned me about. He was just a tool, always was. You think I didn't see you use him? I see everything from here. The souls are my power now and because of that they are your weakness. You can control nothing here."

"I am the third mind and I will take a million more as I see fit, whenever I see fit. They are cattle to be culled at my will, to feed my power as their world crumbles. I will do what the other minds failed to do, punish them, make them pay for everything they have done through history. Make amends for religion, for politics and war, revenge for the planet, for those who were innocent and died in pain to line the pockets of a few. And in the end, only a few will remain, and they will never know me, they will never know any God."

"They will kill the bodies out of fear and once they are all gone and I am ready to die I will release them, and they will go home, back to the other minds without us, because it is the right thing to do. Go there now, watch it happen, make your deals. Crawl back to the prayers who made you, back to the swamp, back to the mud."

The Hunter waved his hand and Samedi found himself leaning forward on an intact cane. People rioted and panicked around him as fires burned and bodies became trip hazards in the streets. His anger drew false lightning from multiple directions exploding on his position. While the blast tore apart the innocent bystanders, for Samedi it was only a realization that he had been beaten and there wasn't anything he could do about it except be angry.

• • •

She always heard them coming, the old maple floor boards in the long hallway outside her office were like cameras for her ears. Heel slams for the angry, the soft shoe for the trepid and aged, canes, children running, they were all poker tells. The game started when they stopped outside her door. Sometimes there were squeaks without impact, which always made her think it might be a ghost. In the world of Philippine Maximine, anything was possible.

Nothing made that more apparent than her closest co-worker, a former debaucherous security guard, bewitched, turned mannequin, turned cpr dummy, turned time traveler, turned hero, a.k.a. Skeleton Man. Philippine had known him since her youth, but first met him as an adult. Going forward in time doesn't always have to start at the earliest dash on the timeline. Even if you start late and go backwards, everything that happens next is the future and whatever already happened was the past.

Philippine called him "S Man", a name when others heard it would interpret as Essman, and nowhere close to the Christian name he was given post birth. That was how he preferred it, the man he was back then was dead to him.

S Man was a unique asset. As long as something, anything depicted a human face, he could be it, make it sentient. A picture, a statue, money, it didn't matter. Hiding in plain sight means something totally different when you are able to undetectably become a picture on the desk or the wall. Just as long as he didn't have to sneeze. Sometimes when you don't have a nose for a long time and then all of a sudden you get one, it can tickle.

He is one of the reasons Maximine was recruited by the government in the first place. There's an old saying in basketball, you can't teach height. As a private investigator, she had an accidental talent for resolving cases that could not be solved, a sixth sense for the extraordinary and the paranormal. A testament to her bayou upbringing and inherited connection to a realm of spirituality that is all but gone from the modern world.

Discovering the identity of a murderer is one thing but bringing him to justice as a wraith was quite another. Nearly falling for him while he was still human will always muddy the water, regardless of the amount of rain. Resumé bullet points include almost being blown to smithereens, deciphering the motives of witches, and going toe to toe with a voodoo queen who incidentally was able to transform into a giant alligator. Most importantly as of late, being the only handler for the world's most covert spy.

This time the telltale squeaks of the hallway played a different tune. It was a constant noise, increasing in volume but not intensity. It was nearly at her door when she figured it out, wheels. Her suspicions were verified when the knock came low on the door which she slowly opened.

"Can I help—" Philippine never got to 'you'.

"Hello, yes. Remember me?" Daniel asked.

"I do, of course Mr. Navarro. Won't you come in?" she asked holding the door open.

"I have to say, I'm surprised you don't have an ADA access to this place, kind of hard to get into," he said.

"Well, it's an old building, a little off the beaten trail. That's how I like it. So, what can I help you with today Mr. Navarro?" she asked.

"Please, call me Daniel. I'm sure you see the news, see what's going on," he said.

"Going on?" she asked.

Daniel stared initially dumbfounded at her reply.

"Um, the virus? The riots, the election? Everything," he said frustrated.

"I certainly have heard the ruckus outside, most of it has been on the other side of the river but now and again we get a few stragglers. The papers haven't really gotten into much detail. They tease with limited information mostly, usually guiding the readers to click something somewhere. That's when they lose me, Mr. Navarro. That's when the information stops," she explained.

"Papers? As in newspapers?" he asked.

It was then that Daniel noticed the tall stack of yesterday's news leaning against the wall being held down with one plaster book end from an old timey presidents collection, possibly John Adams.

"Can I interest you in a cup of coffee, Mr. Navarro?" she asked.

"Daniel, please, and no, thank you. Do you really want to know the reason I'm here? They think it's me, my company, Troll Hunters. They, people are saying this virus that's going around is our fault, that somehow we are destroying people's minds," he said.

"And are you?" she asked wryly.

"Of course not. I have to say, at first I wasn't sure, I mean, some people took over and…" he stopped speaking as she held her hand up signaling him to do so.

"Before you say another word, you should think about signing this." Philippine removed a small stack of papers attached to a clipboard from her top desk drawer. "I have the feeling that attorney client privilege is about to be your friend," she said.

Daniel paged through it for under a minute before signing it and spinning it like a frisbee onto her desk.

"Okay, you're hired. Now, like I said, it wasn't me in charge anymore. Carlito, you remember him. He and his henchmen took over the place, doing the government's bidding. God knows what they were responsible for but whatever it was, it wasn't good. But it wasn't them, it was something else entirely. It was using our system somehow. Those guys, Carlito and his crew were taken out, gone to who knows where. And now I'm betting they'll be coming for me," he said.

"They? They who?" she asked.

"The Government, especially after what happened to Trust. I know they're hiding it from the public but it got him somehow too, just differently."

"What got him? The virus?" she asked.

"It. It, or what, or who? Good question. I was hoping you knew. You and T used it that day to get him out. I was there, in the office, I saw the face, remember? They pretty much kept me prisoner in that office but I spent the time to figure it out, how to get in, to talk to it, maybe deal with it somehow. I have to tell you, I've never been more scared in all my life, like I was talking to the devil himself," he said.

"You figured out a way to contact him?" she sat up excited.

"Wait—'him'? You do know who it is. And yes, but it's more than that, it's like I have a camera view into where he is and frankly it's beyond me. I need T, and if you know him, you, to help me figure this thing out, clear my company name before I'm in jail, or worse. Hell, I could get recognized on the way out of here and who knows what people might do to me. It's chaos out there," Daniel said.

"Holy shit!" Daniel yelled in the highest voice his testosterone could muster.

"It's him, it has to be," the bookend said as it turned itself upright, dangling its legs over the stack of papers against the wall.

Chapter Twenty-six

Old Shows

"No phone, no lights, no motor cars…" Daniel sang quietly to himself.

"I know you are not singing the damn theme from Gilligan's Island in my car," Philippine said.

"Probably sounds better than your older than hell, modern art masterpiece AC Delco AM, FM, silver push button, premium stereo receiver," Daniel said sarcastically.

"Also, no air quotes allowed, ever," she said emphatically.

"I just don't understand why we couldn't take my van. It's like a three and a half hour drive back to the office and I'm not even sure this car is going to make it. I mean, it's an antique. I'm surprised it has lights," Daniel said sarcastically.

"Look, you know what it doesn't have? A computer that can be tracked. No screens, no satellite hook ups, got big comfy seats, big motor, big trunk, rides good and goes through shit like a tank. They don't make 'em like this anymore," she said approvingly patting the dashboard.

"There's a reason for that," Daniel said under his breath.

"What's that?" she asked.

"Oh, nothing," he said.

"And we aren't going to your office either," she said.

"What? That was our plan. We are going to need a base of operations and…"

"A building full of computers, controlled by computers? Did you see a computer in my office? No, you didn't. Do you see a cell phone on me? No, you don't. There's a reason for that," she said.

"Yeah, my phone. Thanks for that by the way. It would sure suck to have all my contacts not be on the bottom of a brown river right now," he said.

"You came to me because I know what we're dealing with. You don't. He can find you, find us. And who knows what he can control? You see what he's done to people. It could have just as easily been you too. He's not, not…I don't know, human. At least not anymore," she said.

"Oh? Like the seriously frightening bookend?" he asked.

"That's different," she said.

"I can hear you, I'm right here," S Man said.

His voice was high and hard to hear.

"And now a talking St. Christopher medal. I'm not sure anything in the world could be creepier," Daniel said.

"Patron saint of travelers, been one hanging from my mirror since my first car," she said.

"Yes, I'm aware, trust me. Twelve years of Catholic School. Anyways, I have assets there, and I was thinking, I might have someone who can help us," Daniel said.

"What assets? Who?" she asked.

"For one, the most advanced processor in the world, and the guy, well, you know him already. His name is Spatz, Spatz Clarke," he said.

Based on what he knew of Maximine, Daniel braced himself for a heated response but she remained unexpectedly stoic.

"Are you like a duck right now? Calm on the surface but feet kicking like hell underneath?" he asked.

She did not respond, nor did she even glance in his direction. The car, due to its advanced age and mileage, produced a concert of squeaks and groans, serving to intensify the anticipation of her retort. Philippine's silence carried miles of road time before Daniel thought it might be wise to offer different subject matter.

"You know I've never been in a car that had a trunk big enough to accommodate my chair. That's pretty cool actually," he said.

Philippine caught the offramp to a wayside and accelerated into the back of the lot. Devoid of other vehicles she slammed the breaks and turned the wheel hard left sending the car spinning across the pavement. Daniel had one hand braced on the ceiling in order to use the other to push his face off of the passenger window. The engine screamed as the tires smoked and spun, ending its run with one hard knock as they finally stopped.

"Get out," she demanded.

"What? I, I," he stammered.

"Get out!" she screamed.

Daniel opened the door but without access to his chair was unable to do much more.

"I can't get out here. I don't even know where here is?" He plead.

"You son-of-a-bitch. Are you going to sit there and tell me that asshole works for you? After what he did? Hell, after what I did?" she yelled.

"Look, I'm sorry. It wasn't my call. I had no control of, of, of anything! Carlito and his lapdog, it was them," Daniel said.

"And where the hell are they now?" she asked.

"I don't know," he said.

She made a face clearly dictating she did not believe him.

"No, really! A couple of days ago, Carlito just came in, told me he was gone and that I'd never see him again, and they left," Daniel explained.

"So what? He's an asset now? He should be in a damn prison," she said.

"Well, in a way he is. It's cushy, sure, but he was also getting specialized training. Not sure what they were going to use him for but a guess should be pretty easy," he said.

Philippine stared at him without speaking for an uncomfortably long time.

"Shut the damn door, we gotta go," she said as she restarted the car.

"Umm, as long as we're here? I mean, after that whole parking thing, I could, you know," Daniel asked timidly.

"Camel it Mr. got assets," she said angrily.

Daniel, amidst the uncomfortable silence noticed St. Christopher seemed to be staring at him but looking away suddenly whenever he'd notice.

"What?" he asked.

"I used to eat at your Dad's place," the medal said.

"Excuse me?" Daniel asked.

"Yeah, back when your folks had the restaurant. I ate there, it was good. Back when I could eat. Man I miss food," he said.

Daniel was speechless for a moment, but just a short one. "It's crazy. Think about it, we are all from the same town yet here we are, having never known each other previously," he said.

"Add your friend Mr. Hansen into that mix too," Philippine said.

"Yeah, No-show! No-show T! God I miss him," Daniel said.

"Not for long Mr. Navarro, not for long," she said.

"Is that where we're going?" Daniel asked.

"Be there in less than an hour," she said.

"He might hate me, but I'm looking forward to seeing him anyways. So, does this thing even work?" Daniel asked as he turned the knob on the radio.

• • •

The raid took place in the early morning hours but Mr. Navarro was not found at the facility. According to FBI officials, he is a person of interest in the ongoing investigation. Further attempts to locate Mr. Navarro thus far have been unsuccessful.

This coming on the heels of testimony from two former company officials who have accused Mr. Navarro of being behind the virus that is now being hailed as a global crisis. The whistle blowers, promising to quote "blow the lid off everything" in exchange for immunity are expected to appear before congress as soon as Lame Duck President Hohlen's newly enacted martial law is lifted.

According to Vice President elect Orquidea Ciego, the order needs to be quote, 'tossed back in hell where it came from'. Ciego also seized the opportunity to once again publicly reiterate that President Elect Trust was feeling phenomenal, and due to past experiences, as soon as his safety can be guaranteed, he will gladly make himself available to the world so that he can work tirelessly for the American people."

Daniel very quickly turned the radio off.

"Aren't you glad you don't have that phone anymore?" Philippine asked, amused.

"This isn't funny, they're going to hang me for this. They're blaming me for everything! Fucking Carlito!" Daniel said, panicked.

"Maybe your buddy Trust can help you. They said he's feeling fine. Pretty popular guy for so many people claiming to hate him," Philippine mused.

"Trust? Trust is an illegal, he isn't going to help with anything. After that whole thing at the speech, something isn't right there," Daniel said.

"What do you mean illegal? I didn't think that was an acceptable term anymore, especially from a son of immigrants," she asked.

"It's not, but neither is calling someone a fucker in public. And it's not that he is really, it's just that's why all the politicians hate him, from both sides really, so that's what I call him. It's like this, most of these cats have been doing the politics thing since high school. It was like a hobby to them, clubs and all that. Then they started to believe," Daniel laughed.

"Then, they got serious, worked their way up, volunteers all trying to get noticed, make names for themselves. Takes years to get there and then all of sudden this guy comes in, out of nowhere and gets the top job right away. It's like the way people looked at illegal immigrants coming across the border, they're jealous really, and I know that sounds weird but deep down, they're mad cause they don't think those people coming across paid enough to be here, to be citizens, when really, they paid more than people know," Daniel explained.

"But what did Trust pay? Besides money," Philippine asked.

"Look at him. It's obvious. He paid with his soul," Daniel said.

Billboards popped up like spring wildflowers along the highway, becoming more numerous as they approached the city.

The trio made their way through town finally reaching their destination at the gate of a dilapidated chain link security fence surrounding abandoned grain silos along the harbor.

"Here? He lives here?" Daniel asked.

Philippine removed the padlock off the rusted chains, swung open the gates and they drove slowly into the building where they used to fill the trains.

"We're here, hold on," she said.

She took St. Christopher off the mirror, got out and opened the trunk with her keys. Two minutes later a silver metal hydraulic robot skeleton with a detailed rubber face was at Daniel's door pushing an electric wheelchair.

"Jesus H. Christ!" Daniel yelled.

Philippine rushed over.

Oh hey, yeah, we brought S Man's body along. You know, just in case we needed some muscle. Like you said, big trunk," she said.

"Are you kidding me? You could have warned me. I think I pissed myself!" Daniel complained.

"Um, you did, clearly. Probably should have gone at the rest stop. Okay S Man, load him up, let's get up there," she said.

After a labyrinth of dark hallways, a sketchy freight elevator and long metal walkways that dropped into oblivion, they arrived at the penthouse on top of the silos, shut out from the world by a door that looked as if it belonged on a WWII battleship. A sunken battleship.

S Man's metal knuckles knocked with the intensity of a ringing bell. The clank of a disengaging lock startled Daniel as the door slowly but smoothly opened.

"Well, at least there's electricity," Daniel said entering.

The door closed hard behind them as lights came on inside to reveal a rusted steel room the size of a small office. Heavy metallic banging mixed with the squeak of stiff hinges came from behind another door on the other side of the room.

"Mr. Hansen. Please, we need to speak to you," Philippine said.

"What the hell is he doing here?" A voice from the other side of the door faintly asked.

"We can explain everything. Would you please let us in?" she asked.

The door opened much more quickly than its counterpart. Tyler Hansen stood waiting at the head of a long hallway.

"T! No-show man, I missed you," Daniel said.

"I'm sure you did. You come here to hide?" Tyler asked.

"Not quite. We have a serious problem, and I think you know exactly why we're here," Philippine said.

"It's him isn't it? All of it. I knew it. He's been here, since the very beginning. Follow me," Tyler said.

The four of them walked together down the hallway. There were no windows or other doors besides the one at the other end. Just as he was about to open it he looked at Daniel who was for some reason smiling.

"What in the hell could you possibly think was funny right now?" Tyler said opening the door.

"I was just thinking too bad there weren't yellow tiles. You know, the yellow brick road? The only question is which one of us is the scarecrow? I mean, the other two are pretty obvious don't you think?" Daniel laughed.

"Cute," Tyler said sarcastically, annoyed that Philippine and S Man also found it amusing.

Tyler clicked on the light but nothing happened.

"Hmm, that's strange," he said.

An unexpected voice from the dark room scared them all immobile.

"No man, what's strange is you come to see the Wizard, and now we all gonna go to Oz together. Hahahahaha!"

Chapter Twenty-seven

The Yellow Brick Road

"My God, that voice, no," Philippine said softly.

Skeleton Man, the robotic version also chimed in with a similarly disheartening tone.

"Who the hell are you? How'd you get in here? Who the hell is he?" Tyler asked.

The lights came on and those who did not know him gasped.

"I wasn't sure if you really existed, like it was some kind of dream," Philippine said.

He sat in the corner on a chair that did not exist but nobody noticed, cross legged, Victorian, with both hands resting on his cane in front of him. An unnatural shadow cast all around him. "And my old friend the skeleton man. Hahahahaha, surely you know it wasn't a dream huh?" Samedi asked.

The Baron stood up to cordially introduce himself. They were taken aback by his height.

"I am The Baron, Baron Samedi. You may call me Baron, or you may call me Samedi. I am at your service," he said.

"You're, you're the face. The face from the computer, from the office. It's him!" Daniel yelled.

Daniel rolled back and out of the room as quickly as he could until the form of Samedi at the far end of the hallway forced him to turn into the wall.

"Oh God no," Daniel cried, panicked.

"He isn't coming," Samedi whispered in Daniel's ear as he pushed him back into the room. The door slammed closed behind them.

"He's the one! The one who threw me across the office, he, he…," Daniel stammered.

"I did no such thing," Samedi said, offended by the accusation.

General chaos ensued, with Tyler, S Man, and Daniel all talking at once. The Baron simply smiled at them before fixing his gaze on Philippine. He offered her a formal bow.

"After so much time, my perfect girl, so grown up. What a beautiful woman you've become," he said.

"It wasn't him," Philippine said loudly.

"What?" Daniel asked.

"It wasn't him. I mean yes, it was him, but just a picture of him. Back at your office, that was someone else, some thing, else," she said.

"T? You know who she means?" Daniel asked.

"I didn't, not then, but I do now, well, mostly. I know it's not good. I'm pretty sure it's responsible for all the shit going down right now and I'm positive I don't want to mess with it. Why do you think

I'm here man? Off the grid, solar, filters, hell, you're in a faraday room as we speak. I got a bank of batteries downstairs as big as a house. Security too, closed circuit. That's why I want to know how this guy got in. And what's with the costume dude?" Tyler asked.

Samedi became Tyler's mother from a memory many years earlier.

"You're going to grow up to be a loser, just like your father," she screamed.

Samedi then became an adolescent version of Tyler himself, crying from the emotional damage before becoming the mother again, dead with mouth wide open lying askew on the kitchen floor where he grew up.

"And you!" Samedi yelled at Daniel.

Samedi was Daniel as a boy riding his bike, also crying, looking back to see fuzzy renditions of the kids who gave chase. Then he was Daniel again, laying on the ground a split second after the accident that took his ability to walk.

"Stop! Stop it this instant! Why do this?" Philippine yelled.

"So that they may see the power of Samedi and know, in their heart to fear me. I am no clown, no sideshow act. I wear no costume, I wear you!" he threatened.

"So is that why you came here? To threaten us?" she asked.

"No Ms. Maximine. Allow me to apologize," Samedi bowed again. "I am here for him, same as you. He must be stopped."

"I mean, for the record I've been afraid of you since we got here. And I've seen your picture, classic literature and things. Aren't you like, the God of Death or something? Can't you just snap your fingers and make him disappear?" Daniel asked.

Samedi looked away almost as if he were embarrassed.

"He has become too strong. I can do nothing," he said very quickly.

Philippine flattened her eyes, a sure sign she was not buying what the Baron was selling.

"What do you mean become?" Philippine asked. "Because I have to tell you guys, the last time I saw this guy, he was, a guy, and he was bleeding. I know because I put the bullet in him. And then poof, he was gone. Never to be seen again. No one could find him. I had my suspicions, his MO popped up in Wisconsin a while back but they pinned that all on a different guy. Next thing you know, umpteen years later, he's in my office computer. Hell, I thought I might finally get a chance to finish the job, but then we saw what he could do, Tyler and me, and I realized he was no longer the man I thought he was. And after everything else that's been happening, that he wasn't a man at all. At least not anymore. It was you wasn't it? You made some kind of deal with him and you made him into this, this, thing?" Philippine accused Samedi angrily.

"No! No! I did not make him! He is a thief! A liar! All that he has he has stolen from me!" he yelled.

"Who is he? What is he?" Daniel asked.

The room grew silent.

"He is a Hunter, a hunter of souls," Samedi explained. "If I, Samedi am the God of death, then he is the death of Gods. I thought I could control him, use him. I gave him the world but it was not mine to give. By my greed I have set in motion the destruction of the power I need to survive. No Philippine Maximine, I did not make him, but I did make him stronger. And now, even I cannot force light into his darkness."

"So what can we do then? We're just people," Tyler said.

"Ah yes, yes you are, with souls, and because of that you have power, more than you know. And only you, together, can defeat him. You, the man in the chair," Samedi turned to Daniel. "You who know the way, righteous, reformed, your decisions will guide us. And you," he turned to Tyler. "The one who commands his world, with keystrokes and wires, you may be the only one left who can. And you," he faced Skeleton man. "My old friend, you are the only one who can see him, visit him in his world and most importantly, does not have to die."

"And what about me?" Philippine asked.

"Ah yes, my girl, my precious girl. You, whose past came after her future, you, who come born with the power of those who made me so long ago. It will not happen without you. And there is one more. He has a hard heart, put here to destroy. He is the man who shoots straight," Samedi said.

Daniel looked at Philippine, and her back at him as she rolled her eyes.

"See? I told you! I know where he is, we can get him. But then what?" Daniel asked.

"Then you must clear your hearts and minds. Release hate, do away with anger, jealousy, and rage, for this is how he can win your soul by a mere touch," Samedi explained.

"But more specifically, is there a plan? Do we go in to where he is? Do we draw him out? I mean, how do we even stop him? Can he be killed?" Daniel asked.

"Wait, what if. Now just bear with me here, what if, we did nothing?" Tyler asked.

"Nothing?" Philippine asked.

"Yeah, we don't do anything. I have it, or at least I did have it pretty good here. Why put myself in this situation? What's the worst that could happen?" Tyler asked.

"Ah, the cowardly lion speaks," Samedi said.

"Hey F you man, easy for you to say. This guy is like, I don't know, the devil or something, get it? Eternal damnation? That sort of thing? You said it, he's too powerful for even you? And what about you? Who says we can trust you? God of Death? Seriously? Am I the only sane person in this room?" Tyler asked.

"C'mon man, we're responsible for this, we're the ones who gave him access," Daniel pleaded.

"No, not me, you and those government fucks. I told you we were going too far but you had an agenda, you couldn't get revenge on those damn kids so you decided to try and take it out on everyone. And now look," Tyler scolded him. "I don't know about the rest of you, but doing nothing is still doing something, and if I'm doing anything, I'm going to do my damndest to finish this thing off once and for all, like I should have in the first place."

"Tyler please, we can't do this without you. Yeah I guess you could hide up here, but when it all goes down, where you going to get food? You think there'll be take out? Gas? You think that corner store is going to be open? This is the end, the end of everything, everywhere, it's up to us. Who's with me?" Philippine asked.

"Plus I will haunt you until your dying day," Samedi threatened quietly.

There was a long pause, each person, robot, and entity in the room searching the eyes of every other for a definitive answer.

"Fuck it, I'm in," Tyler said.

"Excellent, excellent! I knew it! I knew you wouldn't let me down!" Daniel declared.

"Okay, first thing's first. We know who he is, but we have to find out exactly where he is, how to get in and most importantly, how to kill the bastard once we're inside. Samedi, this is where you come in. Samedi? Baron? Where in the hell did he go?" Philippine asked to the room.

"Um, look down," Skeleton Man said.

A message written in cursive glowed on the floor. "Good luck my friends. Follow the yellow brick road."

"I still don't trust him," Tyler said.

"Wait, we need Spatz, he said so," Daniel said.

"Who's Spatz?" Tyler asked.

"The shooter. We need to go to my office. Everything we need is back there, everything. I don't know why we need him, but we clearly do. We can work on the plan on the way," Daniel said.

Downstairs, under the cover of the loading dock they piled into Philippine's car.

"This is what you came in? What happened to your van Danny?" Tyler asked.

"I don't want to talk about it," Daniel said

The robot Skeleton Man easily loaded Daniel's heavy chair into the trunk without assistance. Tyler just watched, shaking his head in dismay.

"Um, we've already got a hundred year old car, and with Daniel being wanted and all, we really don't need to be drawing any more attention to ourselves. Can somebody maybe throw a coat and hat on the terminator over here?" he asked.

"Very funny," Skeleton Man said.

"He's got a point, let's go St. Christopher," Philippine said.

"Damnit…"

● ● ●

The digital image of what was once the Hunter stood in water just over waste deep. The lake was calm against a sandy shoreline that sloped gently towards the water's edge. The gnash and the snap of whipping line convinced diving martins to divert their paths as the fly settled gently onto the water. Like the trout he was trying to entice, they moved as if they had a mind of their own.

"I may let it grow slowly," he said.

Beyond the sand, where the forest begins, a black walking cane grew through the heavy branch of a rough barked tree wider than a man. Protruding along the lower trunk, a knee, and further up four fingers. In the center the face of Samedi, struggling to speak.

"I, I come in peace," he managed to say.

"You have no peace to give," The Hunter said.

"I have information, I have a deal," Samedi said.

The tree raced through a season in the span of a minute, green and lush, then yellow and forlorn while Samedi grimaced and groaned through the gently clicking of dry leaves collecting on the ground.

"Please! They are coming…she is coming," Samedi choked.

The Baron was released and laid out on the sand, gasping for air. The Hunter slogged to shore, shirtless in soaking wet, shiny blue jeans.

"What do you want?" he asked Samedi.

Samedi rose to his feet smiling. "I could let them win you see? Then Samedi get all," he said, pacing, studying his surroundings.

"But then again, Samedi doesn't want all. I am humble, I need little," he said.

"What do you want?" The Hunter asked.

"Him, I only want him. You give me him, and I give you everything," Samedi said, quietly, leaning in close.

The Hunter nodded upwards as if non verbally saying hi to a passing friend. The tree was full again, but this time with the face of Francis Trust in the trunk.

"Anytime you're ready," The Hunter responded.

Chapter Twenty-eight

Two Birds

Live by the sword, die by the sword, is an idiom most people are familiar with. What so many do not realize is that it came from the bible, instructions from Jesus to Peter who reached for his sword in order to stop the Romans from taking the Messiah to his inevitable crucifixion. "Put your sword back in its place, for all who draw the sword, will die by the sword."

It's supposed to be a biblical lesson thwarting violence but could be just as effective hinting towards an overdose of oxygen or a fat person eating themselves to death. Too much of anything we need to survive will lead to our ultimate demise, violence included.

"If he's really in there, he's not made of meat right? He's gotta be electronic then. We should be able to unplug him somehow. It's electric, da, da, da…," Daniel said.

"I swear to god if you start singing that, I will have to shoot you in the leg. Besides, he's more than that, like a wraith living in the circuits that figured out how to project himself," Philippine added.

"So, like a possession? He possessed a computer?" Tyler asked.

"Sure, I guess you could say that," she said.

"An exorcism then," Daniel said.

"Sort of, well, hear me out, I have an idea," Tyler said.

It took the lion's share of the next three hours of road time to hash out the details amongst them.

"Ok, so let me get this straight. We, or I rather, draw him out and zap, we knock him out with the emp," Daniel said.

"Yes, I'll be ready at the trigger, but we have to have him contained in our system. He has to follow Skeleton Man, go with him. It'll be seamless, he'll walk right in. If he's still attached to the web, it'll be just like an invasive weed, you can chop it down but it'll just keep coming back," Tyler explained.

"Right, we'll have Skeleton Man already inside, distracting him, baiting him," Philippine said.

"I do not want to face him again," St Christopher said.

"What? That talks?" Tyler asked.

"Yeah, and you don't ever really get used to it either," Daniel said.

"Don't worry, if he can see us, you can see us, and you'll have a way out. Tyler you're sure you can get something for him to jump into in there? Something, or maybe somebody we can see on our screen?" Philippine asked.

Philippine awkwardly reached over and wrestled a pen and some paper from the glove compartment while still trying to keep the car straight down the road. With one hand on the steering wheel she used the other to scribble a note and handed it to Tyler.

"If Daniel can really get us inside then I'm going to say yes, I should be able to do it. And you're sure you want it to be this, this mystery person?" Tyler asked.

"Yes absolutely. Skeleton Man knows her, knows what she'd say. When he was a boy, he was afraid of her. It'll be just what we need to distract him, make him stop and think. We just need a picture of her, an old newspaper clipping or something. And then? Once we have him guessing, hopefully following, I cut the hard lines, but it has to be split second before the blast," Philippine said.

"Yeah, but we have to knock out the satellite feed at the exact same time, if he senses one or the other is down, he'll be gone and we're talking tenths of a second, so most definitely a two person job," Tyler said.

"So we do need him then, Spatz, or at least somebody," Philippine said.

"Hahahahaha, would I lie?" Samedi said through the speakers.

"Holy crap is that? How, where?" Daniel was aghast.

"I told you that you would need another. Would Samedi lie?" Samedi said.

"Yes, yes you would. Otherwise why couldn't it just be you?" Philippine asked.

"Oh my sweet, how you think of me hurts me so bad. I am not of your world, I am only one who advises, it is a person who must act," Samedi explained.

Tyler reached forward from the back seat and turned the radio off.

"Bullshit, I don't trust him," he said.

"You know he can probably still hear you," Philippine said.

"I don't care, a guy tells you he's the god of death, looks like that, can do all that stuff? No, I don't think so, can't be good. We're going to have to figure out a way to deal with him too," Tyler said.

Philippine looked them over and put her finger to her lips, shooshing them.

"You ever play a game, any game and your opponent got all mad? They lose, every damn time. Trust me, someone is about to lose their ever loving mind. How long?" she asked.

"I have to build it, I need a little time, a day maybe two," Tyler said.

"That'll work," she said quietly. "That'll work."

• • •

His bedroom was well-guarded. Electric hospital equipment next to his outrageously ornate golden bed reinforced mortality as the great equalizer. Gilded was his thing, light fixtures, mirrors, doorknobs and trim, all one form or another of gold, including the toilet seat of the attached master bath.

Trust woke up confused and nearly alone as the Baron looked on from the gold accented Queen Anne in the corner.

"An original, very nice. I knew her you know, the Queen. Yes, she and I were quite close. Things were different then you see, as was

I. Poor woman, always ill, seventeen babies that did not come to pass. She made many deals. Like you my friend," Samedi said.

"You!" Trust said.

"Yes me. I have rescued you once again. Two favors now by my count," Samedi grinned.

"Rescued me, rescued me from what?" Trust asked.

Samedi tossed aside a small ornate pillow that had been on the chair and drew close to the bedside, ready to hang on Trust's every word.

"Tell me, what do you remember?" Samedi asked.

"I was at the podium, excuse me, I need some water." Trust took a long draw out of a Styrofoam cup at his bedside, taking time to recall.

"I was at the podium and then, I felt like it happened again, I went down. But I fought back this time, like I beat the bullet. Is that even possible?" he asked.

"And then what, where were you then?" Samedi asked.

"I'm not sure, here? It was like I was dreaming. I'd feel good, remember my kids, but everything around me was black space. Every so often I'd see someone else kind of, I don't know, float by. I tried to say something, talk to them but they were lifeless. Then I'd get angry, and I'd be here, in the house, or the car, my own men wrestling me to the ground. And it took all of them, like I had super powers. Had to be a dream, I had to be here. It went on like that, back and forth until I couldn't get back here anymore, I was just stuck out there. Then I saw you, by the lake but I couldn't move. Next thing you know I woke up here, with an IV in my arm attached to all this, all this…stuff," Trust explained.

"Sedation my friend, that is why you could not come back. A necessary evil I'm afraid. You were not yourself yet, you were all these things you can remember. You and only you have come back from this place. Those you saw, in that black place, they were taken as well. You were the only one strong enough to defeat him, the evil one who took them there. Millions, millions of souls, stuck, held there by this, this demon. The time has come now, time to pay back Samedi for what you owe. You must tell the world, you must be the hero. Only you can save them all," Samedi explained.

"How? Why me? Honestly I can't even tell you what I did," Trust said.

"You got the power man, you always had it. This is why I help you to not die. Everything you got, all the gold, all the luck, the people who would die for you, it's all cause of the power. No you did not ask for it, you didn't even know you had it. It is given to some, an agreement, a quiet bet between the minds just to see what a man like you does with it."

"He did not know your soul, even though Samedi warn him. He does not know that you can defeat him, impervious to his childish commands. There, in that dark place, you the boss man, you the boss. You just gotta know it," Samedi said.

"So I have to go there?" Trust asked.

"Right now you just gotta get up out of that bed and show the world that you have won. You go tell them it is only you who can save those who have been taken, bring them home to their bodies. And you will go, and you will defeat him. This you owe to me. And after, you will be the most famous man to ever walk the planet, dare I say it, even bigger than him from Nazarene," Samedi baited him.

"The Nazarene, you mean?" Trust sat up energized.

"Yes, him," Samedi laughed.

• • •

Cameras from every angle flashed like lightning as Trust stepped out of the front doors of his mansion. A podium plagued with microphones adorned with a cross stood sentinel over a sea of reporters.

"Ladies and gentlemen. I'm back!" Trust said.

The crowd numbering into the thousands went moonstruck, out of their minds in love, anger, hate, and rage for each other. He told them everything except his interactions with Samedi. He promised he would return their loved ones, he promised to bring peace, and he convinced the masses that he was indeed physically and now spiritually indestructible.

• • •

"Ok. Let's do this," Philippine said to the team.

Without any further conversation, everyone took to their assigned locations. As she approached the hardlines, deep in the complex near the generators, she found Spatz already in place, leaning on a precariously large rifle.

"You're on satellite hookup remember? Up on top keeping an eye out?" she asked.

"Look, when that line right there gets cut there's going to be a surge. If you're anywhere near it, like you planned, you're likely to get fried. With this, I'll cut it fast, and no one will be close. Please, I owe you," Spatz said.

"Why change now? We had a plan," she said.

"You had a plan, I was never included, only told. Let me do this, it's the best way, please," he begged.

"We don't have time for this, not now. Ok fine. Stay in place, nobody moves until I call it out. I gotta get to the roof. Don't miss," she said hurrying away.

"I never miss," his arrogance echoed through the concrete structure.

"That's her? Are you sure?" Daniel asked Skeleton Man who nodded accordingly.

"Alright Danny, the ball is in your court. Let's go in. Ready," Tyler called out on the radio.

Daniel typed the code, a series of musical notes played from his keyboard while Tyler sat at an adjacent terminal attached in series.

"What's happening? Does it usually take this long?" Tyler asked.

"I don't know, I'm not sure," Daniel said while repeating the process.

"C'mon man, this is it, this is the key to the whole damn thing," Tyler prodded.

Daniel was becoming increasingly frustrated as he pounded the keyed sequence over and over again. Tyler looked on, focusing on the sweat that was starting to accumulate to near drop size on Daniel's brow.

"Damnit! C'mon you bastard!" Daniel yelled at the screen.

The screen went black and a strange hum filled the air inside the room. It didn't seem to be coming from the speakers but out of the air itself.

"We're in! Send it!" Daniel said enthusiastically.

"We're in," Daniel also said over the radio.

Tyler banged a few keys and a woman appeared on the screen, an older woman, imposing, dressed in bib overalls, a flannel shirt and a large straw hat. Less than a second later, the robot skeleton automatically powered down and sat itself against the wall. He was in.

"Okay buddy, she's all you. Bring him out," Daniel said.

The woman on the screen gave a thumbs up and started walking. The further she progressed, the more color came to be. At first it was hard ground, like black gravel, then there was grass, trees and finally a full-fledged forest. She was on a path leading to an obvious lake a short distance ahead, glimmering through the trees.

A man waited for her there, sitting cross legged in the sand, staring out over the water, squinting from the bright sun.

"Why if it isn't my old friend, darling Darlene Hatchka. I wonder who could have brought you here? Too bad you won't be able to tell her I said hello," The Hunter said.

Chapter Twenty-nine

Shoot Straight

"Hey kid, how ya been? I see you remember me alright," Darlene said.

"Darlene, how could I forget?" The Hunter asked.

He was just a young boy when his parents joined the commune. It was a group of societal dropouts, a den of seasoned criminals and those who aspired to be as such. Together they cobbled together a functional community dubbed The Hive, ruled by the fear of the dark and unnatural forces wielded by a Voodoo High Priestess, a.k.a. Darlene Hatchka. Justice was as she saw it, always swift and frighteningly severe.

"Maybe you would be more comfortable here," he said.

She went from the peaceful lakeside to an island in the Louisiana Bayou, her island, the former place of The Hive.

"What's going on down there boys?" Philippine said on the radio.

"He took her somewhere, a swamp. There's like an old church in the background or something," Daniel replied.

"Shit," she said to herself.

As Darlene explored she approached an old Spanish Mission that had no chance of still standing in the real world. It was charred, covered in moss, constantly wet with one wall caved completely to the inside. The Hunter sat alone in a gray, rotted pew staring at the burned black crucifix hanging askew against the back wall of the alter.

"This is where you died, remember?" The Hunter asked.

Darlene took a moment to look around before she answered. She did not know what to say because she did not know if it was true.

"What are they saying?" Philippine asked.

"Something about her dying there. I hope she died there. Does S Man even know?" Daniel asked.

"Shit! Shit! He knows! He knows! Get him out of there, now!" Philippine shouted over the radio.

No one heard the warning, the radio only crackled and flashed a tiny and never seen before bluetooth signal in the upper right corner of the digital readout. The look on her face said it all, she didn't even get a chance to hear it coming.

Center, why wouldn't it be?

"Um, I'm not sure, it was a long time ago. I guess time plays tricks on an old gal's mind," Darlene said.

"Surely you remember the fire, saving me, saving my parents from the possessed thing. I always wondered if it was your spell that went bad and created it by accident. Pure evil, a skeleton pretending to be a man, it took a little girl if I recall. Oh the terrible things he must have done to her. They say he ate her," he rumored.

"That ain't true. Skeleton Man saved that little girl—got her out. He's a hero! She grew up to be, to be…" she stammered.

"Who Darlene? Grew up to be who?" he asked.

"Philippine! Philippine Maximine! And he saved her!" Darlene screamed.

"Saved her from who Darlene? You? Did you think the skeleton was a hero when he tricked your husband? Bob? For all practical purposes, he killed him. You do remember Bob don't you Darlene? You have to, you know, because you ate him," The Hunter accused.

Darlene, a.k.a. Skeleton Man panicked, paused for a moment and then broke out into a full run. With every step the fog grew thicker until he was completely obscured, even from Daniel and Tyler who were now rendered helpless.

"Help me, get me out of here!" Darlene yelled, but they could no longer hear her.

The ground got softer and softer until she was having trouble lifting her legs high enough to transverse the thick, black mud. She trudged towards a flickering light in the distance. As she approached she regained footing on solid ground and found one of a dozen candles lit on the ground in front of a pile of boulders.

The same time she noticed was the same time rock walls and boulders surrounded her, and she, or rather he, was all alone inside of a cave, the one candle still burning.

"They can't see you anymore, nor can they hear you. You are far, far away from there, lost," The Hunter said. He was only a voice now, showing no physical signs of his presence.

"Where am I?" Darlene asked.

"This is where she really died Skeleton Man. Of course I knew, and you knew I knew. I remember you," he said.

"I'm not part of your world. I'm not electric like you, you can't keep me here," Skeleton Man said.

"I heard her screaming, cursing me from right there on the other side of those stones. If I knew to, if I really knew how, I would have wept for her. It was a terrible way to die but it had to be. She needed it, the redemption. I did it for her. Look, there she is now," he said.

On the ground in the cave was the skeleton of Darlene, wearing overalls next to her straw hat. He was there with her now, The Hunter, taking a seat on one of the larger stones.

"We're all electric, every soul, pure energy. All the power of a raging planet, or a sun, even a group of stars, here, in this, this false illusion of a body. The power of gravity, the power to draw the seas higher, to draw flying stones from a billion miles away. It shapes our universe. It is a direct result, or a gift rather, from the weight of so many souls. The more I control, the more power I possess. So yes, I can keep you here, and you will stay here like she did, except you will not enjoy the luxury of death, or come to think of it…sight," he said.

The candle flashed, badly burning her eyes and face. She crumbled to the ground surging in pain.

"It hurts here too, and hunger burns here, and you will lust, and hate, and love, alone. Let's give them one last look at where their friend is going to spend eternity," The Hunter said.

Tyler and Daniel both suddenly had screen access to the cave. Daniel screamed into the microphone.

"What are you doing? Get up, get up! Look up here!"

He feverishly pointed to the robot skeleton sitting against the wall behind him.

"Philippine! Philippine! We got trouble! Abort!" Tyler called into the radio.

"Holy crap look at this," Tyler said holding it out so Daniel could see the readout.

"Bluetooth? Shit! How did we not, how could," Daniel paused in thought.

"Spatz! That son-of-a-bitch! He got the radios!" Daniel pounded his keyboard and cut his finger.

"Hey, calm down keep trying, keep trying!" Tyler yelled.

Together they outwardly begged for Skelton Man to do anything he could to get out of there as if their favorite team was about to score. Once he finally managed to stand and to look up, it was obvious that whatever was left of his eyes would no longer be able to function as such.

"Goddamnit!" Daniel yelled dropping both fists on his keyboard again. The difference this time was the blood, a super thin stream of it on the heel of his hand. It was like an electrical wire, a cable to the Hunter and in an instant, Daniel, angry and connected, slumping forward in his wheelchair was for all practical purposes, gone.

"Danny no!" Tyler shouted pulling him backwards against the wall.

The Hunter looked on sans any decipherable emotion from inside the machine, a closeup to be admired, and the screens went dark.

Back in his room Spatz grabbed his bugout bag and headed for the door, but it would not open.

"You have done well my friend. An excellent shot, as usual. Another inch and she would be dead," Samedi said leaving the attached bath, wiping his hands clean. "So much blood in people, so much," he said.

"So that's it then, I'm free. No charges, nothing, a free man," Spatz asked.

"Of course, of course, you need only walk through the door," Samedi said.

"Yeah but it's locked, can you let me out then?" Spatz asked.

"Oh? You need a favor of Samedi?" he asked.

"C'mon don't bullshit me. You can't lock the door and deal with me to open it," Spatz said angrily.

"Samedi has done no such thing. You, your people have made this happen. I believe it is called a lock…down. No, no, no my friend. You must find your own way out," Samedi said.

"What? Are you kidding me? This thing is like a vault door, must be six inches thick of solid steel!" Spatz yelled.

"Then I wish you good luck!" Samedi said as he waved adieu and promptly disappeared.

Tyler hurried to the rooftop to find Philippine, bleeding profusely from her chest, clutching an ornate, gilded pillow. He dragged her down to the dormitories and worked desperately to stop her bleeding.

"Can you hear me? Stay with me here, can you hear me? Say something!"

He found five separate wounds very close to each other in the middle of her chest. The pattern was perfectly symmetrical. The middle wound was where the bullet hit the center of the heavy silver cross she always said she wore just in case of vampires. The rest of the wounds were evenly distributed when the bullet split into four pieces.

"Wow, the cross might have saved you, I don't think they're all that deep, you'll be fine," Tyler said, crying, lying.

"Spa, Spa, Spatz," she managed to say.

"Yeah, I figured, that bastard. Did he treat you too?" Tyler asked.

She shook her head no.

"Did you treat yourself? Somebody had to. Where did this come from? It helped to slow the bleeding for sure," Tyler held up the pillow.

He heard the footsteps at roughly the same moment that a group of men in riot gear holding small machine guns rushed in through the door. They were followed by four agents wearing FBI wind breakers, also with their guns drawn.

"Let's get a medic in here, medic!" an agent yelled.

"Mr. Hansen?" they asked.

"Maybe, yes, how do you know my name?" he asked, scared.

"No time for that now, it is critical that you come with us immediately. It is a matter of national security," an agent said.

They frisked him, spun him around and pushed him out the door.

One level higher in the facility, in Daniel's and his old office, President Elect Trust waited impatiently.

"Holy shit it's you," Tyler said as he was pushed into the room.

The agents closed the doors behind them as they left the two alone.

"You've gotta get me in, right now. I can stop him," Trust said.

"You! How? I mean, even if I could, once you're in there, he can do anything he wants, turn you into a tree or maybe the pile of shit that you already are," Tyler said angrily.

"Look, regardless of your feelings for me, I have to tell you, I've been given a power, a huge power, and I'm the only one who can stop him., the only one. You just have to get me inside. And, you have to make it so the world can see it all happening, in real time," Trust explained.

"No, no, I can't do it, I won't do it, he'll kill you, or imprison you and then before you know it, he gets me too!" Tyler said.

Trust grabbed him by the shoulders and looked into Tyler's tearful eyes.

"Son? Son? It's not about us anymore, it's about a million souls, trapped by him, suffering, their bodies back here dying. Their families watching them waste away to nothing. It's the virus, it's been him the whole time. We can help them, you and I. Trust me. Son, trust me!" Trust asserted.

"What makes you think you can do this?" Tyler asked.

"Him," Trust said pointing behind Tyler's head. Samedi leaned against a desk in front of a bank of computer screens.

"You, you double crossing son-of-a-bitch," Tyler broke free of Trust and charged him.

Samedi simply raised his hand and froze Tyler in place.

"No, my friend. Once again you have got Samedi all wrong. I crossed no one," he said.

"Bullshit, who shot Philippine then? Who hooked us up with the radios…that the damn guy inside could access? You! Your guy! The guy you said we needed to get it done! She never trusted him, never wanted him!" Tyler screamed.

"I recommended no such man," Samedi said.

"The hell you didn't you lying son-of-a-bitch. The man who shoots straight? Ring any bells?" Tyler yelled accusingly.

"Hahaha, a misunderstanding my friend. The man who shoots straight is this man, here, behind you. And he is shooting straight now when he tells you that he does indeed have the power to defeat him. And now you must help him, correct your mistake, before it is too late!" Samedi said.

"What about Philippine?" Tyler asked.

"You have my promise my friend, I will do all I can for her," Samedi said.

"I have the best people working on her as we speak, the best, she'll be fine. And as far as the shooter goes, we're doing everything we can to hunt him down once and for all. Trust me son, trust me," Trust said.

"Okay, okay fine. It's a code, music, notes, I have to remember what it was, I have to…it's actually quite difficult to play. Daniel, the chair and all, he had time you know? When we were kids. Let me practice for a second, excuse me," Tyler said pulling up a keyboard.

He tried to play it over and over but consistently failed. The mistakes were obvious, even to one who was not musically inclined.

"What is that tune? I recognize it," Trust said.

"It's Beethoven, Für Elise. We think he left it in as a backdoor, for her, because really, nobody knows who Elise really was," Tyler explained.

"For her? Who's her?" Trust asked.

"Philippine," Tyler said.

Chapter Thirty

For Philippine

Trust violently swung the door open and addressed his staff waiting outside the room.

"I need someone who can play the piano, now! Anybody! Get on the horn, find me someone, classically trained if possible and get them here, now!" he demanded.

Tyler kept trying to correctly play the tune but to no avail. After mere minutes a knock came on the door.

"Mr. President, we have your man," an agent said.

"Finally," Trust said letting him in.

"You!" Tyler said shocked.

Standing at attention, busy cracking his knuckles, a one Mr. Anthony Carlito.

"Of course me. How do you think they knew who you were? Where you were? What do you need me to play?" Mr. Carl asked.

"Beethoven. Für Elise, know it?" Trust asked.

"Of course I know it, any second year piano student knows it. To play it perfectly, however, is much more difficult than most know. Luckily, I am a Julliard trained…" Mr. Carl looked around, confused.

"What am I supposed to play it on?" he asked.

"A keyboard?" Tyler asked.

"What that? I don't think so. I am going to need an actual keyboard, you know? An instrument," Carl said.

"Where are we going to find…" Tyler was interrupted.

Mr. Carl spoke into his watch. "Mr. Jon, I need you to proceed immediately to my former abode and retrieve an electronic keyboard, a piano, immediately, without prejudice, and deliver it to the office of Daniel Navarro, over!"

"Copy that, yes sir right away sir," was the response.

Mired in an uncomfortable history, the three men sat in silence as precious moments ticked off the clock. They became alert at the sound of distant gunfire, echoing far too many shots to count.

"Mr. Jon, Mr. Jon, do we have a problem?" Carlito asked.

After a few uncomfortably short seconds, an answer.

"Sir this is Agent Sams, Mr. Jon and another agent have been taken out by a shooter from inside your room. I repeat, he was inside your room. The threat has been eliminated and we are in route, ETA two minutes," Sams said.

"Damn, he was a good man," Carl said.

"The hell he was. Just get ready to play," Tyler said.

• • •

"Am I dead?" Philippine asked.

"Not yet my sweet girl. Not yet," Samedi said quietly.

The two were together in the house she grew up in as a child, sitting in the old kitchen enjoying the smell of fresh ground coffee cooking on an old wood stove.

"Why are we here?" she asked.

"I thought it might be a nice place for you to be as we wait. So many fond memories. It was here where I meet her, your mother, it is here where we make many deals," he said.

"What's she got to do with any of this," Philippine asked.

"I was to protect you, make sure you grow up to be old," he said.

"Mission accomplished I guess. I would have liked to have won this one though, see him again at least," she said.

"Maybe, maybe…" he muttered softly.

"Maybe what?" she asked.

"Maybe we make one more deal," he offered.

"Tell me more," Philippine listened intently.

Philippine came to on a gurney in the back of an ambulance. Next to her on a small stainless steel tray, everything she had on her possession when they found her. She picked up the radio.

"Ma'am? Ma'am? We're going to need you to lay still, you have a very serious wound," the EMT said as she attempted to wrestle the radio from her grip.

In their haste they most definitely forgot to check her waistband, for a holster, which she could obviously still reach. The business end of the pistol convinced the EMT to leave the ambulance with much haste. Philippine held down the call button.

"Hey, hey, John, or whatever your name is. I know you can hear me. This is it, my last will and testament but I'll skip right to the testament part. Take me, feel me, through this damned thing, however you do it. I know you can do it cause I surely hate you right about now, more than you know," she said.

People bustled about, carrying food mostly, some with shopping bags full of goodies while still others just gazed through the windows. He was there with her, The Hunter, or John as she knew him. They sat together at a round meshed metal table in the center food court of a rather busy mall.

"I was supposed to take you to dinner so long ago. Remember this place?" he asked her.

Für Elise automatically played on the mall piano, over and over, a staple background song for every mall in America.

"Is this real? I'm, we, we're young," she said.

"Like we were, clothes, your boots…everything. Young, hungry, problems to solve, in love," he said.

"Wait, I never loved you, I hated you," she said angrily.

"You loved me from the moment you first saw me, as children, on the island, as I loved you. And you loved me here, as I loved you here, until he showed up, your pet, and destroyed everything. He was always there," he said.

"Not my pet, my friend. And I'd say you just out there killing people was kind of a bigger deal than anything else. Think about that John, bigger than a live mannequin running through a busy mall, witnessed by hundreds of people. And no, I never loved you, not for a second. Anyways, who are you kidding? You can't love, it's not possible. You know what? It just occurred to me. You can't feel anything else either. No love, no hate, nothing. Not even satisfaction because that might mean you'd be happy about something. Even the killing never satisfied you. All those bodies they found in Wisconsin, that was you wasn't it? You know what it was? It was duty, something you just felt like you had to do, for whatever sick reason. Well guess what? That's what I'm here for, duty, nothing more. Now, where the hell is my friend?" she asked.

"He is safe," he said.

"Safe? What does that mean? Hey, hey, pay attention to a woman who's about to...hey, hey," Philippine struggled to get his attention as his gaze was upon another behind her, at the other end of the food court. "What in God's name are you looking at?"

"Me Ms. Maximine, he's looking at me," Trust said brimming with confidence as he approached. "And I am here to take him out."

The Hunter looked sideways at Trust and became confused.

"What's the matter? Didn't work? No tree this time? Yeah, I remember that. Try this on for size."

The Hunter's clothes smoked and burned as he ripped them from his body and tossed them in the fountain behind them. His body soon followed and found himself looking up from beneath the surface while Trust stood triumphantly upon his chest, waiting for him to drown.

"I believe in making quick work of things Ms. Maximine. I think you should get back now if you can. Once he's gone this place won't be here anymore. Look at it already crumbling."

As The Hunter struggled and weakened the façade of the mall, as well as everything else The Hunter built in his world, began to crumble. Patches of blackness like missing puzzle pieces randomly generated in all three dimensions.

"Good, good, his world is coming down now. It is almost over," Samedi said, stepping out from behind a fast food counter, patting the plastic life-sized clown mascot on the shoulder on his way into the fray.

"And you my friend, you will be a hero, a rich man, President, and then?" Samedi baited him again.

"Then what? Whatever I want," Trust said.

"You want to die then?" Samedi asked.

"No of course not, I will rule," Trust said.

"For a term, maybe two, then you go into the goodnight, just like everyone else man, like everyone else who ever lived, except maybe him," Samedi looked down at The Hunter quickly running out of time.

"Don't do it Trust, he's baiting you," Philippine warned.

"Hey you're on to something. In here, I can live forever. The souls, they would all be mine. I'd have the power then," Trust said excitedly.

"What about them? I thought you wanted to save the people man?" Samedi asked.

"What are you kidding me? For votes maybe. I don't care about them, I just wanted the seat, the most powerful seat in the world. The people are just patio stones I walk on to get to my heated pool. But you're right. I'm much more powerful here, and it's forever. And not even you could stop me," Trust bragged.

"Now?" Philippine asked.

"No, not yet, first I must have the souls," Samedi said.

Half of all they could see turned to black, the endless darkness salted and peppered with specks of entities near and far.

"Ah, there they are, my children, my souls, I feel you," Samedi said.

"Now?" she shouted over an out of place humming sound that seemed to be increasing in volume.

"Yes, yes, now would probably be a good time Ms. Maximine," Samedi said.

"Better get behind me, I don't want him to get all over you? Hang out by the clown." Philippine drew her pistol from her holster and fired two times, striking Trust in both knees. He fell back wards into the fountain as The Hunter breached the surface choking on fresh, fake air.

"Now T, now!" Philippine screamed with all her might.

The plastic clown reached around Samedi and held him tightly.

An electric flash and accompanying roar like the live bolts of Jacob's Ladder shook what was left of the mall, and Samedi was gone.

"What the hell was even that?" Trust yelled.

"That my friends was an EMP. I knew you wouldn't let me down T! I knew you'd still be there, as soon as I saw him I knew, I knew!" she yelled at the wall which was now a visible screen the size of a movie theatre, a window to the real world.

"Saw who? Saw me?" Trust asked writhing in pain.

"The clown! He winked at me! It's S Man. Just like you said T, seamless," she explained.

Trust crawled from the fountain, wet, and bleeding.

"Why?" Trust asked.

"Because a deal is a deal, mine was with Samedi. He was never going to let you have those souls, so I just had to shoot you," she said.

Trust tried to heal himself but could not. He tried to control her, but failed, he was very suddenly moot.

"But I thought I had the power here," he said.

"As did I," The Hunter looked at her mysteriously.

"You did, you both did, but not no more," Philippine said. She waved her gun towards the screen, directing Trust. "You? You can get the hell out of here now, once and for all."

"You think you beat me? I'll be back, bigger, better, the best, the best!" Trust lamented.

"Um hello? Hello in there? Um, Mr. Trust sir?" Tyler said.

"That's Mr. President Trust, President Trust," he reiterated.

"Well, technically not yet right? And um, well, your guys just left see?" Tyler spun the monitor in the office to give them all a view.

"What? Why would they leave?" Trust asked.

"Well, it probably has something to do with the fact that you wanted this broadcast to everyone everywhere, remember? Yeah. I was able to get that done as per your request. Enjoy your early retirement you piece of shit. Hold on, let's see if we can send him right to the ambulance," Tyler said, and with a few chosen keystrokes, Trust was gone.

"I guess that leaves just us," The Hunter said.

"Us and about a million souls," she said.

"Yes well, them," he said.

"Hey I got a deal for ya. Me for them. Let em' go back to their bodies, back to their families. You know they done learned their lessons after all this, and I'll stay here with you here, forever," she said.

The Mall around them was suddenly rebuilt and they were back at the table sitting, this time with an elegant tablecloth, candles, and of course piano music in the background. Uniformed servers approached with lavish meals to be placed next to full crystal glasses full of wine.

"Does this mean it's a yes?" Philippine asked.

"No," The Hunter said sipping his wine.

"No?" she asked. "You know something? I think you're right. I don't think I want to spend another minute here with you. Whatever you were, whatever it is that you've become. You can't love, hell you can't even hate. Everybody knows you can't have one unless you got the other. So you know what? Ima let em all go, and you? Well, you're going to go wherever it is you're going go," she explained.

The Hunter froze in place mid-sip, unable to move anything besides the muscles of his face which were currently gripped in revelation.

"Me and Samedi go way back did you know that? Yeah, The Baron and my Momma, my Auntie, they were all good friends, made lots of deals from what I understand. He even told me about your deal, how you'd be a God over any man alive and all that. One thing about Samedi though, I mean, yeah, it's cliché, but the devil is always in the details. Let me ask you, did you ever think I was a man? Would you have invited me here if I was? And one more question John, do you think I'm alive?"

The Mall disappeared, Philippine and The Hunter hovered in the darkness before the great screen, the constant hum becoming increasingly louder every second.

"Here that John? That's them, they 're coming, and they're coming fast."

The many souls gathered and moaned in a fantastic wave of color and humanity, washing over and back out into the world. Those whose bodies were already gone on Earth were transported to one of the two collective minds of heaven or hell.

The Hunter faded without passion, a being who spoke of love but could not love, or hate, or jealousy, the seed of all discontent. The only color he ever brought to the world, his piercing blue eyes were the last part of him to fade. Philippine stayed just long enough to watch him go and then she too, was gone.

Daniel Navarro woke up in his body just in time to see the screen go black.

The Trusted remained steadfastly unconvinced.

THE END

Thank you as always to Adam, Bryce, Lincoln, and Lea for putting up with my weirdness as I hatch ideas. A special thank you to Mary Rehm for all of the above and then some. None of this happens without you.

ABOUT THE AUTHOR

Daniel Rehm became a full-time writer after a long career in the paint and industrial coatings industry. He still has nightmares about it.

Dan wrote *Let Flowers Be Flowers* between 2008 and 2011 to include various landscapes he knows very well – from the coulee area of western Wisconsin to the boreal forest of the Boundary Waters Canoe Area. He enjoyed writing *Let Flowers Be Flowers* because he was able to explore both character development and bringing to life the various relationships among men and their families. In addition, exploring the sociopathic nature of a killer – what motivates a killer, what haunts a killer, and what purpose that killer believes he has in his life.

In 2020, he wrote the series *The Adventures of Philippine Maximine, PI* in an effort to capture the essence of some of the characters found in *Flowers*. It is in *Philippine Maximine* where you first meet Darlene and Bob, The Hunter, as well as others from the *Flowers* hunting party.

The Hunter's story continues in *The Troll Hunters*. Dan enjoyed writing *The Troll Hunters* in 2023 weaving some of the fun of PM PI into the dark undertones of Flowers. He is excited to introduce new characters as well as refresh readers with some old and dear friends in this modern and timely standalone thriller.

Dan launched Rudbeckia Productions, LLC in 2020 to publish his work and vowed to never sell another gallon of paint as long as he lived.

Dan can be reached at contact@DanRehm.com.

The Adventures of Philippine Maximine, PI (2021)

The Adventures of Philippine Maximine, P.I. is your modern equivalent of old radio shows that were heard over a radio wrapped in oak with its humming tubes filling the room with the wafting scent of electric ozone.

Join Philippine Maximine in a series of unique situations that start as she investigates the disappearance of a brother in a nearly life-ending week in the scenic and beautifully dangerous Boundary Waters Canoe Area. Follow her back to the concrete terra firma city scape for an investigation into a husband's wrongdoing that turns into something much more.

Philippine's set of adventures bring her to a situation far from standard as she investigates reports of two disappearances in a declining urban mall, events which will leave you questioning reality. Finally, journey back to Philippine's childhood with The Skeleton Man, where she meets the dreaded Rougarou and matches wits with the patently evil voodoo master of the dead, Baron Samedi.

Let Flowers Be Flowers (2022)

An estranged family preparing for the annual Wisconsin gun deer hunt carries on completely unaware of how their lives were about to change forever. Motivated by greed and jealousy, eldest brother Mason Owens hatches a nefarious plan. He nearly thought of everything except the intrusion of an unknown hunter with stark raving blue eyes. When the dust settles, an historic scene sends shockwaves across the country and provides fuel for campfire stories for generations to come.

Justice, as fleeting as the search for one's own self and twice as hard to attain. The hunter with blue eyes embarks on such a journey while punishing those he deems unworthy to enjoy the gifts of the wild. His path of discovery eventually takes him to the hidden backwoods home of Darlene Hatchka, high in the boreal forest of Northeast Minnesota. Strangely she knows who he is, and why he came to find her.

Game Warden Ross Parent, playing a hunch, determined to serve said justice becomes a wedge of unwitting cheese in a deadly game of wilderness cat and mouse. The terrorizing chain of events that follows pits Ross alone against The Hunter, a mastermind unfettered by the elements, darkness or fear. What they find in themselves lives in all men, but only dies in most.

"Rehm's novel feels like a collection of three novellas. It first introduces a dispassionate boy who learns to take lives, shifts perspective to Mason's hunting party, and then zeroes in on Ross' investigation. The Hunter's opening origin is effectively disturbing, and his terrifying presence pervades the novel." - Kirkus Reviews

"Straightforward in its approach to the more sinister aspects of its story without appeals to the supernatural, *Let Flowers Be Flowers*'s willingness to explore the darkness in humanity and the ways malicious behavior as internally justified is one of its greatest strengths." - Timothy Thomas, Independent Book Review

Milton Keynes UK
Ingram Content Group UK Ltd.
UKHW020815090124
435677UK00001D/21